LOVE IS
FORGIVING

Novella looked at Sir Edward and a sudden tenderness sprang into her heart.

"You seem to understand how I feel about Crownley Hall – " she murmured.

"It is obvious to anyone who meets you that you love the Hall as much as you do your Mama and Salamander!"

Sir Edward laughed as he patted Salamander on the flank, as he was grazing contentedly on the river bank.

It had been a long time since Novella had felt so happy – and she found herself completely at ease in Sir Edward's company.

Novella was well aware that she had little experience of dealing socially with the opposite sex outside of friendship. There had been a few would-be suitors who called at her lodgings at the school, but her maid had always sent them away, saying she was not at home.

Novella had never been in love and she could not imagine what it might feel like.

But standing on the riverbank, watching Sir Edward playing with Salamander, she felt a mysterious yearning in her heart that she could not explain.

'I must not indulge myself in silly notions,' she thought, shaking herself. 'I must not allow myself to be distracted from Mama and Crownley Hall.'

Nevertheless, she could not deny that she felt a strange, haunting longing and a secret thrill at being in Sir Edward's company.

"We should be moving on," she suggested, drawing Salamander close to her, "will you please help me up?"

THE BARBARA CARTLAND PINK COLLECTION

Titles in this series

1. The Cross of Love
2. Love in the Highlands
3. Love Finds the Way
4. The Castle of Love
5. Love is Triumphant
6. Stars in the Sky
7. The ship of love
8. A Dangerous Disguise
9. Love became theirs
10. Love drives in
11. Sailing to Love
12. The Star of Love
13. Music is the soul of Love
14. Love in the East
15. Theirs to Eternity
16. A Paradise on Earth
17. Love Wins in Berlin
18. In Search of Love
19. Love Rescues Rosanna
20. A Heart in Heaven
21. The House of Happiness
22. Royalty Defeated by Love
23. The White Witch
24. They Sought Love
25. Love is the Reason for Living

LOVE IS THE REASON
FOR LIVING

BARBARA CARTLAND

Barbaracartland.com Ltd

THE BARBARA CARTLAND PINK COLLECTION

Barbara Cartland was the most prolific bestselling author in the history of the world. She was frequently in the Guinness Book of Records for writing more books in a year than any other living author. In fact her most amazing literary feat was when her publishers asked for more Barbara Cartland romances, she doubled her output from 10 books a year to over 20 books a year, when she was 77.

She went on writing continuously at this rate for 20 years and wrote her last book at the age of 97, thus completing 400 books between the ages of 77 and 97.

Her publishers finally could not keep up with this phenomenal output, so at her death she left 160 unpublished manuscripts, something again that no other author has ever achieved.

Now the exciting news is that these 160 original unpublished Barbara Cartland books are ready for publication and they will be published by Barbaracartland.com exclusively on the internet, as the web is the best possible way to reach so many Barbara Cartland readers around the world.

The 160 books will be published monthly and will be numbered in sequence.

The series is called the Pink Collection as a tribute to Barbara Cartland whose favourite colour was pink and it became very much her trademark over the years.

The Barbara Cartland Pink Collection is published only on the internet. Log on to www.barbaracartland.com to find out how you can purchase the books monthly as they are published, and take out a subscription that will ensure that all subsequent editions are delivered to you by mail order to your home.

If you do not have access to a computer you can write for information about the Pink Collection to the following address :

Barbara Cartland.com Ltd.
Camfield Place,
Hatfield,
Hertfordshire AL9 6JE
United Kingdom.

Telephone :   +44 (0)1707 642629
Fax :   +44 (0)1707 663041

THE LATE DAME BARBARA CARTLAND

Barbara Cartland who sadly died in May 2000 at the age of nearly 99 was the world's most famous romantic novelist who wrote 723 books in her lifetime with worldwide sales of over 1 billion copies and her books were translated into 36 different languages.

As well as romantic novels, she wrote historical biographies, 6 autobiographies, theatrical plays, books of advice on life, love, vitamins and cookery. She also found time to be a political speaker and television and radio personality.

She wrote her first book at the age of 21 and this was called *Jigsaw*. It became an immediate bestseller and sold 100,000 copies in hardback and was translated into 6 different languages. She wrote continuously throughout her life, writing bestsellers for an astonishing 76 years. Her books have always been immensely popular in the United States, where in 1976 her current books were at numbers 1 & 2 in the B. Dalton bestsellers list, a feat never achieved before or since by any author.

Barbara Cartland became a legend in her own lifetime and will be best remembered for her wonderful romantic novels, so loved by her millions of readers throughout the world.

Her books will always be treasured for their moral message, her pure and innocent heroines, her good looking and dashing heroes and above all her belief that the power of love is more important than anything else in everyone's life.

"Love is the reason for living, and it is certainly the reason for everything else in the universe as well."

Barbara Cartland

CHAPTER ONE
1871

"Excuse me, my Lady, but Mrs. Palmer wishes to see you at once in her office."

The maid bobbed a curtsy and Lady Novella Crownley put down her book with a sigh.

'I wonder what she can want,' she thought to herself, as she walked down the numerous corridors to the Headmistress's office.

The past few years had been difficult for Lady Novella. After having been a pupil at the Chelford School for Young Ladies, she had stayed on as a tutor after her father, the Earl of Crownley, had died.

Her mother had said that it was for the best that Novella remained at the school until such time as the Earl's complicated estate had been settled.

Novella was an only child and a girl at that, and so her inheritance, in law, was definitely not automatic. It was with utter relief that she had received the news that her father had left a watertight will naming her and the Countess as joint beneficiaries.

But that was eighteen months ago – so why, wondered Novella, was Mrs. Palmer summoning her to her office? The occasion reminded her so much of that day when she had imparted the dreadful news of her father's sudden death, and Novella hoped fervently that she was not about to tell her that her mother had passed away too.

So it was with a shaking hand that she knocked on the oak door of Mrs. Palmer's office. After a long moment, she bade her enter.

"Ah, Novella, thank you for coming so promptly."

She paused and took out a pair of eyeglasses that she immediately placed on her nose.

"I have received a letter from your mother."

"Not bad news, I trust?" asked Novella, her heart in her mouth.

"For you perhaps not, but for Chelford School, it is not the best of news."

"I am afraid I do not understand."

"Your mother asks that you be relieved of your duties at Chelford school in order to return to Crownley Hall."

"Does she say why in the letter that it is now the right time for me to return home?" asked Novella.

"I am afraid that there is no further information in her letter," replied Mrs. Palmer, taking off her glasses. "But I am certain that you will be happy to be at home once more.

"Novella, it has been a pleasure to have you at Chelford school, but I always knew that your employment here was not going to be forever. The girls will be sorry to lose you – you are popular as well as attractive – and I would like to thank you for your singular dedication to their education. I have made up your salary to the end of the month, but you are free to leave right away should you so choose."

"But the girls – " stammered Novella, completely overwhelmed by this latest turn of events, "I should like to say – my goodbyes to them."

"In that case," announced Mrs. Palmer, standing up, "I would suggest that we make arrangements for you to leave tomorrow after assembly. That will give ample opportunity for you to take your last class this afternoon and to pack up your belongings."

The tall woman moved towards Novella and in an uncharacteristic gesture, threw her arms around the young girl and embraced her.

"You have had a difficult start to your adult life, Novella," she said, releasing her, "but you have shown an admirable strength of character that I am certain will aid you in the outside world. Make no mistake, my dear, living in a scholastic world shields one from some of life's more unpleasant elements, but I am in no doubt that whatever you choose to do from hereon in, you will make a success of it."

By now, Novella was crying. She felt immensely sad at leaving the school – it had provided her with a place of retreat after her father had died as well as invaluable companionship.

Wiping her eyes, Novella left Mrs. Palmer's office. As she retraced her steps along those corridors, she could scarcely believe that so soon she would be leaving them behind forever.

Back in her room, she sat down at her desk and wrote a letter to her mother, informing her that she would be leaving Chelford school just before noon and expected that she would arrive at Crownley Hall late that evening.

She wrote,

"Dearest Mama,

Please be sure to ask Wargrave to have the carriage meet me at the station. I cannot wait to see you all again. I have missed my horse, Salamander, more than I can say and the first thing I shall do upon my return, after kissing you, is to visit him!"

'I do hope that Sally is still at the Hall,' thought Novella, as she began to pack her belongings. 'And Harry and Gerald.'

She thought of all the other staff at Crownley Hall who had served her since she was small. Sally was her personal maid and although Novella had been too young for a lady's maid as such, she viewed Sally as being as good as one. She often gave Sally little presents of clothes that she had outgrown or no longer wanted.

'I shall miss everyone so much, but the time has come for me to go out into the world. Mrs. Palmer is right, I am young and should not be spending my days locked up in a girls school.'

Novella was thinking of love and marriage. Although she had not been in the least bit interested in either since her father had died, she was aware that time was marching on and that it would be to her that the family would look to when it came to supplying an heir.

At twenty, Novella did not realise just how beautiful she had grown – nor did she see the admiring looks she garnered from young men when she walked with her pupils through the town.

'I do hope that Mama is well,' sighed Novella, taking the photograph of her down from her chest of drawers, 'she did not write to me about her health or her well-being, which is most strange seeing as Mama is obsessed with both.'

She smiled to herself at the recollection of her mother calling for the smelling salts at the slightest excuse. She was what her father had described as being 'delicate', so Novella was pleased that she had inherited his constitution rather than hers.

The Earl had been a strong and handsome man, who even in his last years appeared much younger than he actually was. Which is why it had been such a shock when he had fallen down dead after a day's hunting. He was never off a horse and he had brought Novella up in much the same fashion.

'I cannot wait to see Salamander!' said Novella to herself once more, 'it has been so long since I last rode him. I do hope that those stable boys have been taking him out for regular gallops. He gets so cross when he is just left in the field or the stables. Yes, as much as I long to see Mama, I equally long to see my beloved Salamander.'

*

All too soon, the next morning dawned. There had been many tears when she had announced in art class that she would be leaving the day after – and she had been deeply touched by her pupils' reaction.

The last assembly was an emotional affair and many of the girls were openly weeping. They presented Novella with a bunch of flowers and an amber pendant.

A small group of girls was given permission to skip lessons and accompany Novella to the station. She could not have wished for a better send off.

As the train pulled out of Chelford station, she waved her handkerchief, blinded with tears and smoke from the train's engine, until the platform was out of sight.

Settling down into her first class carriage, Novella soon drifted into a reverie, recalling everything that had occurred over the past few years.

She had been a very good student, with the possibility of art school ahead of her, when that awful day came when Mrs. Palmer had called her into her study to inform her that her beloved Papa had died.

Even though Novella was just months away from completing her education, she threw aside all notions of going to art school in Paris and was about to pack up and return to Crownley Hall in Surrey, when her mother had written to her saying that it was best if she stayed put.

'To think I believed that the world had come to an end!' Novella told herself, as she looked out of the window at the passing fields. 'How young and silly I was.'

When Mrs. Palmer had suggested that Novella might like to stay on as a tutor at Chelford school, teaching the girls art and needlework, she had jumped at the chance. Dedicating herself to the girls made her forget her heartache.

'And now I am on my way back home.' she thought, more than a little bit excited. 'But I wonder what I will do with myself now that I am no longer teaching?'

Until the day that her father's will had been settled, Novella's salary was the only income that had kept her afloat.

As a result of having to be frugal, even when she came into her money, she still continued her parsimonious habits. It did not occur to her that she could spend her days shopping for pretty gowns or fine hats, or that she was now rich enough to buy a whole stable of horses.

*

It was nearly dark when the train eventually pulled into Crownley Station. Novella was very tired, as she had needed to change trains twice and take a cab across London to Waterloo.

Stepping down from the train, she was followed by a porter who had kindly unloaded her bags onto a trolley for her.

Novella hardly recognised the station as she had travelled by carriage at Christmas – it was some time since she had last been there and it had been completely renovated. There were flower boxes and a new waiting room.

"Which way is the exit?" she asked perplexed, after finding that the waiting room stood where the old exit had been.

"This way, my Lady," replied the porter, gruffly.

He led her to the front of the station where Novella was surprised and disappointed to find that no carriage stood waiting for her.

"Can I hail a carriage for you, my Lady?" asked the porter.

"That will not be necessary, thank you. My own carriage should be here soon."

"Well, that was the last train through, my Lady, so I will be leaving shortly myself. If you are sure you do not need a carriage, then I will bid you goodbye."

'This is most strange!' she said to herself, hearing a distant clock strike eleven. 'Mama would have guessed that I would have been on the last train and would surely have sent Harry or Gerald to fetch me.'

Just then, she saw a man looming out of the shadows behind her.

"Beggin' your pardon, miss. Do you have the time?"

"Why, yes," said Novella, bringing her wrist up to see her watch more clearly.

What happened next seemed to go by in a flash. The next thing she knew, she was on the ground and her bag had gone.

"Stop! Thief! He has stolen my bag!" she cried.

She started to run after the thief but he had disappeared. There was no one around and the station was deserted. Tears began to stream down her face.

Turning back towards the station entrance, Novella could see that the porter was still locking up the rear gate. Seeing her coming towards him in a state of high agitation, he dropped the lock and ran to meet her.

"Miss! miss! Are you hurt?"

Novella broke into sobs – she felt so alone standing

there and so vulnerable.

"I – I've had my bag stolen and my carriage has not arrived," she stammered, "I do not even have a handkerchief as that was in the bag."

"Here, miss," offered the kindly porter, handing over his large one, "don't you go worrying yourself. I have my horse and trap around the corner as I live outside the town. Let me take you to the Police Station where you can report the devil who stole your bag."

Novella wiped her eyes and blew her nose.

"This is not an auspicious start to my homecoming," she exclaimed. "I live at Crownley Hall and have not been home since Christmas."

"Beggin' your pardon, my Lady. I did not know that her Ladyship had a daughter. I have not been here long – "

"That is quite all right – " She looked at him, questioningly, not knowing his name.

"Jenkins, my Lady."

"Thank you very much, Jenkins. We should proceed to the Police Station at once and then I must make haste home. I cannot think what has detained my carriage, perhaps there has been an accident on the way."

*

And so Novella found herself spending her first hours back in Surrey, ensconced in the local Police Station. The Officer was most sympathetic and offered to take her home in the station carriage after they had completed the formalities.

"I would be glad to accompany you back to the Hall," he said. "for it is late and the road is dark."

Novella thanked Jenkins the porter and made a mental note to recompense him for his trouble. It was nearly midnight by the time that the rickety black carriage pulled up outside Crownley Hall.

Knocking on the heavy door, Novella was suddenly overcome with exhaustion.

"I do hope Wargrave has not gone to bed yet," she said aloud, as the door swung open.

But it was not Wargrave who stood there, but a strange woman!

"Yes?" she said, irritably.

"I am Lady Novella, the Countess's daughter," replied Novella a little put out. "Why was the carriage not sent to the station to pick me up? I have had a terrible time. My bag was stolen by some ruffian and I was forced to beg a ride home."

"Sorry, my Lady, but I was not given any such instructions."

"Where is Wargrave?"

"Who?"

"The butler!"

"I am sorry, my Lady, but he no longer works here."

Novella looked at the woman with surprise. She did not care for her one bit. Novella thought that she had a somewhat sour look about her.

"What about Harry and Gerald?"

"Were they the footmen? I am not sure, my Lady, of their whereabouts."

"And you are?" queried Novella, a trifle irritated at the woman's overweening attitude.

"Mrs. Armitage. I am the new housekeeper."

"Very well, Mrs. Armitage, I shall not disturb Mama at this time of night, I will proceed straight to my room. I had intended visiting the stables to see Salamander, but it is too late now. Is he well?"

Mrs. Armitage looked at her blankly and, after a nervous cough, evaded the question.

"You will find, my Lady, that you have had your things moved to the blue room. Her Ladyship will explain it to you in the morning,"

'What is this?' thought Novella, most unhappy that she had been relegated to what had once been a guest room.

'Half of the staff seemed to have disappeared since Christmas and I am moved into another room?'

Mrs. Armitage led Novella upstairs and along the third landing to her room.

"I have had the room aired and the bed-warmer was put in many hours ago, so I cannot vouchsafe for it still being warm," she snapped.

Novella, remembering her manners, thanked the woman and then closed the door behind her.

The blue room was pleasant enough, but it was not hers. It did not have the wonderful view over the park like her old bedroom and it smelled a trifle unused.

'At least all my furniture and belongings are here,' sniffed Novella to herself, looking up at her carved wooden bed with the huge corona bearing acorns, leaves and the family coat of arms.

'I would have been most upset had I been forced to sleep in another bed!'

It had a special significance for her as her father had ordered it made for her as soon as she was old enough to leave the nursery. She loved it all the more as her parents had identical beds in each of their rooms.

Novella did not waste any time – she undressed quickly and slid into bed. The sheets were still warm and she quickly fell asleep, all the trials of the day soon forgotten.

So exhausted was Novella that she slept right through until the gong sounded for breakfast.

'Goodness, it is late!' she cried, looking at the clock on the mantelpiece.

'Where is Sally? Why has she not come to help me dress? No matter, I will have to do the best I can on my own.'

Running downstairs, Novella's first thought was the joy she would derive from seeing her dear Mama again.

'I will run straight up to her and embrace her,' she told herself, as she raced downstairs.

She was quite out of breath by the time that she entered the dining room. Her mother was already seated, spooning fruit into her mouth. Her eyes lit up when she saw Novella and swallowing her grapefruit, she cried aloud,

"Darling! You are home! We were so worried when you did not arrive before bedtime."

"Mama! Dearest. replied Novella, fervently kissing her mother on the cheek, "I am so sorry but there was no carriage to meet me and then I was robbed at the station."

"Are you hurt, my dearest?"

"No, Mama, I am fine."

It was then that she noticed that they were not alone in the room. Novella's first thought was that it was a new butler, but when she looked again she saw that he was far from a servant – although elderly, his clothes were expensive and tasteful and he wore a large diamond ring on his little finger.

Seeing Novella staring at him, he bowed, and then continued to help himself from the buffet.

"Mama?" she asked questioningly, "you did not say that we had a weekend guest."

The Countess coloured deeply and bade Novella to sit down.

"Darling, I have some news for you."

Novella could not take her eyes off the man – taking in every last detail. She could feel her blood rising, she did not like the look of him one bit!

"Darling, I did not wish to tell you in a letter as I wanted to tell you face-to-face. The fact is that I have remarried and this is Lord Buckton, your new stepfather."

Novella fell back into her chair and gasped,

"Mama! Why did you not tell me sooner?"

"Darling, I was so lonely after your dear Papa died that I thought that I too, would follow him into his grave. Anthony was here for me, right from the day of the funeral and stayed on to keep me company. I have never been alone in my life, darling, I could not bear it! So when Anthony proposed, I accepted."

Novella's eyes were fast filling up. She wanted to shout and rage at her mother – how dare she fill her father's shoes so quickly!

But, being a good daughter, she held her tongue.

"Darling, please do not look at me with those reproachful eyes, I cannot bear it," said the Countess, knowing only too well what her daughter was thinking.

Then she started to cry and Novella thought it only a matter of time before the bottle of smelling salts was called for.

"I want you to be happy and now with two parents once more, you can be," spluttered the Countess, "Anthony has been indispensable in helping me sort out your father's estate and I could not have done it without him."

"Mama, why have I been moved into the blue room and what has happened to Wargrave – and Harry and Gerald?

Why did Sally not attend me this morning? I was forced to dress myself!"

"You are going to have to get used to doing for yourself," interrupted her stepfather, brusquely. "Staff cost money and it's money we do not have, so I dismissed them all. Wargrave was no more than a tottering old fool and was ready to be put out to grass. With just your mother and myself here, there was no need of such luxuries as footmen and lady's maids. As for the room, well, I fancied yours for myself. You were not around and I saw no point in letting such a marvellous view go to waste."

"But Wargrave has been here since before mother and father married," protested Novella, rising to her feet.

"And he ran the house into the ground keeping up such ludicrous appearances," countered Lord Buckton. "I stepped in just in time to stop the whole family sliding into the workhouse!"

"How can that be?" stammered Novella, "Father left provision for both the house and Mama. There were thousands of pounds in the account."

Lord Buckton moved over to Novella and stared at her long and hard,

"Young ladies should not be troubling their pretty, little heads with such affairs. Money is for men to rule over, not women. Your mother lets me have free rein here and I trust I will not encounter any opposition from you on this matter?"

Novella glared back at Lord Buckton, despising the rich, well-fed face, lined with dissolution and recklessness. It was not, she thought, the face of a man of noble character.

She bit her lip and sat back down.

The maid who was now attending the table looked as if she should be in the scullery, rather than waiting at table, but Novella tried not to think about it.

"You will have met Mrs. Armitage?" asked Lord Buckton, as he sat down at the table with a plate overflowing with fish and meats.

"Yes, I have."

"Fine woman. She served in my father's house for many years. Of course, when I came here, she had nowhere to go."

"Have you sold your own house and estate, then?" asked Novella, straining to be as polite as possible.

The Countess coughed loudly and Novella sensed that she had posed an awkward question.

Lord Buckton, however, seemed unperturbed,

"It was a costly pile sitting there doing nothing," he began, carving up the bacon on his plate, "I do not believe in keeping on things for sentimentality's sake, and I needed to realise my assets in order to pay some outstanding debts, so yes, I sold the house."

"Was that before or after you married Mama?" asked Novella, as coolly as she could. Deep inside, however, her heart was thumping wildly. Cold indignation was growing by the second within her bosom.

"Oh, I do not recall exactly," demurred her stepfather, "sadly, Crownley Hall is even more of a drain on the coffers than my own home."

"I trust, my Lord, that you are not thinking of taking Crownley Hall down the same path as your own estates." replied Novella, daringly.

"Darling," interrupted the Countess, sensing that the subject was far too touchy to be discussed, "you know that your father left ample provision for the house and for you. It was made quite clear in his will."

"Ha!" cried Lord Buckton, to the astonishment of Novella, "there is not a will in this land that my lawyer could not challenge if I set him to it."

"What is mine is mine, my Lord," replied Novella, firmly. However, she was inwardly seething. "Father's lawyers were the best and he would not have wanted Mama or me to be in want."

"I am now your stepfather and I think you will find that in law, what is your mother's is mine and likewise, what is yours is mine also."

"Anthony, we should not discuss such unpleasant subjects around the breakfast table," cried the Countess, looking quite pale. "Novella, darling, tell me what you intend to do on your first morning here. The garden, sadly, is not what it should be as we had to let the gardeners go just as it was time for them to start their hardest work."

"I thought that I would take Salamander for a ride. Oh, Mama! I have so longed to ride him again and the day looks set to be fine, so I can think of nothing better than to take him out across the fields and down to the river."

Novella glanced over at her mother and noticed that she was looking distinctly uncomfortable.

"Darling, there is something else I need to tell you – "

"No, Salamander – he's – he's not dead, is he? Please tell me that he is not dead! I could not bear it!"

The Countess looked at Novella and then at her husband. Without warning, she suddenly began to cry.

"Novella! Oh, Anthony. *I cannot tell her*!"

Novella's heart was beating so hard in her chest that she felt it might jump up into her throat and choke her.

"Mama, what is it that you cannot tell me?"

There was a long silence, broken only by the Countess weeping softly.

Lord Buckton did not even look up from his egg and slicing the top off it, he announced,

"What your mother is trying to tell you – quite unsuccessfully due to her delicate constitution – is that Salamander is no longer here at Crownley Hall. He is quite well, however."

Novella stood up, her eyes blazing.

"I demand to know where he is."

"A good daughter does not demand anything of her parents," replied Lord Buckton, his gaze like ice. "For your information, I have sold Salamander and every last decent beast in the stable to a friend of mine. He will not want, I can promise you and I am sure that Sir Edward will allow you the privilege of visiting him occasionally should you throw a pretty smile his way."

Novella was incensed. She rose from the table, shaking like a leaf. Waving away the maid who was just about to place an egg in front of her, she burst out,

"How could you allow him to sell Salamander? Mama, how could you?"

Then she ran out of the dining room and back upstairs.

Tears fell down her cheeks, hot and wet.

'How could he?' she cried, as she threw herself onto her bed. 'Who does he think he is? He is not fit to warm my father's slippers by the fire, let alone usurp him when he has not been in his grave more than two years.'

Feeling utterly wretched, Novella wept for hours.

'This is not the kind of homecoming I had expected!' she sobbed. 'I fear that my very wellbeing is in danger for I do not think that Lord Buckton would hesitate in taking what money I have. I have to protect myself, I have to! Mama seems under his spell and has never been the strongest of characters. Oh, Papa! I wish you were here! You would be horrified if you could see what has become of your beloved Crownley Hall and your daughter.'

CHAPTER TWO

By the time that luncheon was ready, Novella had decided that she must formulate a plan to safeguard her mother, herself and Crownley Hall.

'I must not let my stepfather think that I am a weakling who is easily swayed like Mama,' she said to herself as she splashed her face with cold water. 'He is obviously used to being obeyed and I have no intention of doing so unless it is necessary – he is *not* my Papa.'

Novella was cool and collected by the time she entered the dining room.

Her mother was already there, pacing up and down by the large, picture window that overlooked the front gardens and drive.

"Ah, Novella, dearest, are you feeling better?"

"Quite, Mama, thank you."

"Darling, I am so sorry that you had such a shock about Salamander, but really, he was going to waste sitting in that draughty old stable. He is better off where he is – "

Novella did not reply – she had every intention of paying Sir Edward, whoever he might be, a visit in the near future.

'Probably some old crony of Lord Buckton's,' she thought, dismissively.

"Is Lord Buckton not joining us for luncheon?" asked Novella.

"No, dear, he has some business in London and will not be back until much later."

'Good, I can take a look around the house without him interfering,' thought Novella, as she began to eat the soup that the maid had put in front of her.

"Ugh!" she cried, after one mouthful, "what is this?"

The Countess looked a little embarrassed as she answered,

"It is ox-cheek soup. Your stepfather has cut the household budget since we were married and I am afraid we have to make do with cheaper fare these days."

Novella thought back to breakfast and the enormous pile of meats that Lord Buckton had piled upon his plate.

'Obviously, when it suits him he allows the expense,' she thought mutinously.

"What has happened to cook?" asked Novella.

"Cook has left, I am afraid. We have a new one."

"Did she work for Lord Buckton too?"

"No, dear, she did not. Novella, I do hope that you are not going to take against him – not many would have taken on an ageing woman with an uncertain future."

"Mama, you know that is not true! Father would not have left us in need and I intend to find out precisely what we have, one way or the other. I wish to visit his solicitors as soon as I can."

"But darling, do you think that wise? We do not want to create a fuss, after all."

The Countess rose from the table.

"Novella, I have quite a headache coming on, I think I shall go and lie down. My chest feels like a herd of elephants have been stamping on it – I must have caught a chill during my drive yesterday. I will leave you to your own devices this afternoon, I am certain that you will find much to amuse you."

Novella bent and kissed her mother and then walked over to the window.

She left the dining room and headed for the drawing room. It had once been the scene to many a happy evening spent with her parents – her mother playing the piano and her father singing in his rich bass voice. Novella recalled the songs – some sentimental and some classical.

But a shock awaited her when she entered the room.

'The piano! It's gone.' she cried, running over to the spot where it had stood.

The shawl and candelabra that used to adorn it were now on the mantelpiece, looking shabby and unloved.

Casting her eyes around the room, Novella could see that the walls were in need of repair. Damp patches were springing up underneath the cornicing and around the windowsill and the carpet was so worn in places that it was dangerous.

Novella hurried out of the room and made a tour of the whole house. What she found exhausted and dismayed her. In each room she entered, there were pieces missing and in their place, inferior articles had been substituted.

Going downstairs into the kitchen, it seemed a very empty place indeed now that most of the servants who had previously worked there had gone. A red-faced woman with a rough voice and even rougher hands stood by the range, which itself looked as if it had not seen a lick of grate-black for many months.

"My Lady," said the cook, bobbing a curtsy while wiping her hands on her grubby apron.

"I am sorry but I do not know your name," began Novella.

"Higgins, my Lady."

"How many staff do you have?"

"His Lordship is most particular, my Lady. There is just me and the girl. Mrs. Armitage helps out if it gets busy or I gets meself behind."

"What can we expect for dinner?"

"Lamb chops, potatoes and a selection of vegetables, my Lady, with a choice of puddings. His Lordship has the sweetest tooth I swear I have ever come across."

"Thank you, Higgins."

Novella was fuming as she walked back upstairs towards the West wing. Although she guessed it was now little used, it was where the family would entertain for large dinner parties and also housed several guest suites. Her father had filled it with friends during the hunting season. What awaited her there made her cry.

"Goodness! There has been a fire and nothing has been done to restore it!" she said aloud, as the acrid smell of old, burnt wood hit her nostrils.

Tears filled her eyes as she fingered the charred remains of silk curtains and fine hangings. Everywhere there was dirt and debris. At the far end of the wing, the roof was open to the sky and everywhere was wet and mouldy.

'Why did Mama not say there had been a fire in one of her letters?' she thought, as she hastily retreated from the awful scene.

'I shall go and see Charles in the stables. Even though Salamander is no longer there, it will give me comfort to be amongst old friends and animals.'

She turned the corridor which ended at one of the many exit doors that led out onto the rear gardens. In a few moments, she was heading towards the stable block.

'I fear the worst!' she whispered, for the stables seemed strangely quiet.

Peeping into the stalls, she found that there were still a few steeds left behind – her mother's nag, Bluebell, although now an old lady herself, was chewing contentedly on some hay.

"Hello, old girl," exclaimed Novella, in delight. It pleased her to see at least one familiar animal.

"Miss Novella."

She turned round to see the gnarled figure of Charles, the old groom, standing there holding a sack of hay.

"It does these old eyes good to see you again!"

Novella ran up to him and took his weather-beaten hand, squeezing it hard.

"And I you! But Charles, I am devastated that my stepfather has seen fit to sell all the best horses – Papa would have been seething!"

"Right you are, my Lady," he said, nodding sagely, "ain't been the same since old Salamander left – my only comfort is that he went to a good home, he did. Sir Edward is a fine horseman and loves his beasts almost as much as your father did."

"Well, that is some reassurance indeed to hear you say that, Charles. Who is left in the stables, apart from Bluebell?"

"There's Folly and Mabel – poor old nag – all she's fit for is poking around the fields. And Jasper is still here – but he's an old one too now."

Novella shook her head in dismay.

"I cannot believe that after father had put together the best collection of horses in the County that they have now all gone. It does not seem right."

"That it doesn't, my Lady."

"And are you quite alone now?"

"Apart from a young boy, Ned, who comes up from

the village when I need him. He's a good lad, but he doesn't live in like what I does."

Novella took a handful of hay out of the sack that Charles held and walked over to Folly's stall.

"At least we still have one half-decent horse. Why did they not take her?"

"Sommat about keepin' her for his Lordship's sister to ride when she came. But I've not seen hide nor hair of her yet."

"Then, in future, I shall ride Folly," decided Novella, "now, Charles, can you tell me what has happened to the West wing?"

"Don't know if I should say, my Lady. It is only hearsay after all."

Novella looked at the old groom with her huge, brown eyes in the way that she had so often used when she was a little girl.

"You can tell me, Charles, I will not think ill of you, whatever it is you have to say."

"Well, I heard that it was a party of his Lordship's that got out of hand. Grown men playing silly fire games. But that ain't the worst of it."

Novella raised a delicate eyebrow.

"There is more?"

"I assume my Lady has not seen the Tower, then?"

Charles put down his sack of hay and crossed his arms. His whole demeanour was that of outrage.

"No, I have not."

"Struck by lightning the week after her Ladyship got wed. All the fancy carvings tumbled down into the garden and there they lay still. Cryin' shame, I call it, cryin' shame. Will you be able to do something about it, my Lady? I am so glad you're home at last."

Novella listened to the old man's outpourings and her heart sank into her boots.

"Thank you, Charles. Your candour has been much appreciated. I intend to go and visit this Sir Edward and tell him just what I think of a man who would snatch a dead man's horses from under the family's nose!"

"He be a good man, my Lady, not like most of his Lordship's friends – "

"Then I trust he will be a reasonable man too when I ask him to return my Papa's horses."

"He bought them fair and square, my Lady. He did not know that he was going to be treading on toes."

"You like Sir Edward?"

"Yes, I do, my Lady. He spent many hours with the horses and me before he took them away, finding out their little ways and what they liked to eat and when."

"Nevertheless, he is still a friend of my stepfather's, so I shall reserve judgment until I have met him myself. Rest assured, Charles, I will have Salamander back at Crownley Hall! I will! Even if I have to pay double what Sir Edward paid for him!"

With that, Novella bid Charles one last farewell and returned to the house.

*

At eight o'clock on the dot, the dinner gong sounded.

'At least I shall have a decent meal as my stepfather is at home,' Novella said to herself, as she smoothed back her heavy, dark hair and fastened her diamond necklace, that her uncle had given her for her last birthday, around her neck.

She was not looking forward to another interview with her stepfather – she felt that inevitably, it would turn into an unpleasant discourse about the state of their finances.

'I do hope that Mama is feeling better,' she mused, as

she opened the door of the dining room. 'I shall ask her about her health and will not allow her to distract me with idle chatter.'

Taking a deep breath, Novella entered the dining room. Sure enough, her stepfather was already seated, while her mother flitted nervously around the room.

"Novella, darling."

"How is your headache, Mama?"

"Quite gone now, thank you."

"I saw Charles this afternoon and he mentioned that he thought you had not been too well of late."

The Countess looked a trifle flustered and coughed,

"It is nothing, dearest, a sore throat that is proving most persistent. Charles is a silly old fusspot who behaves towards us all like we were still children."

Novella laughed,

"That is true enough and most refreshing it is too. I would not change him for anything,"

"Such impertinence should not be tolerated in servants!" barked her stepfather, looking up from his glass of claret. Novella noticed that it was already half-empty.

"Charles has been with the Crownley family since the old Earl was alive," replied the Countess meekly, "he came to the Hall as a boy and has always spoken his mind."

"Then perhaps it is time we found another groom," snapped Lord Buckton.

"Anthony, darling, I beg of you, he is the only one left – he is without equal when it comes to handling horses."

Lord Buckton grunted and took another slurp from his glass.

"You are probably right, my dear. All my friends are highly jealous of the way he handles even the most fiery beast – he is worth his keep, otherwise I would have dismissed him along with the rest of that other hapless crew. He is cheap, too. I would struggle to replace him, offering such low wages."

There was a tense silence as the maid brought in the soup.

"Excellent! Hare soup," exclaimed Lord Buckton, picking up his spoon, a look of obvious relish on his face. "Now, tell me, Henrietta, have you managed to transfer some more money from your account into mine?"

"I – I am afraid I was unwell this afternoon and could not travel to the bank," stammered the Countess.

"Henrietta, you know that I need that money quickly. I have to go to London again tomorrow and I need to have the cash. Can I not trust you to do anything right?"

"Mama is unwell," intervened Novella, firmly.

Lord Buckton refrained from eating and looked at her long and hard.

"You have a lot to say for yourself, young lady. As I am paying for your bed and board, I would advise you to keep silent unless I speak to you."

"I have my own money, sir, and if you wish, I will give cook some funds to cover what I am consuming. Furthermore, I had a good look around the house today and I shall likewise be funding some urgent repairs. It must have escaped your notice, with your busy calendar, that the West wing is decaying under our noses whilst the Tower is set to fall down before long."

Lord Buckton's eyes bulged and his face turned red.

"Impertinence!" he shouted, "Telling a gentleman what to do in his own house."

"I think you will find that the house is mine and Mama's," replied Novella, quietly, not shrinking from his gaze.

Lord Buckton looked as if he were about to explode.

"We shall soon see about that. And if you insist on frittering money away, then you can give me some. You will kindly hand over whatever cash you have on you."

"I am afraid I have none, sir. My bag was stolen at the station upon my arrival and it contained all I had. I have need myself to visit the bank."

"You will, naturally, sign over right of access to your account to me."

"I will do no such thing!" retorted Novella, her eyes blazing.

"We shall see about that. We will hear no more of this folly at the table. Henrietta, be good enough to shut off the West wing so that people cannot wander in there as they please," he demanded, his mouth set in a grim hard line.

"Will you be repairing the Tower?" asked Novella, stubbornly.

"And where will I find the money for that whilst I have so many mouths greedily gobbling up my assets?"

"Novella, dear, do not upset your stepfather, he is a busy man and is trying to do his best," put in the Countess, quietly.

Just then, Mrs. Armitage knocked and entered the dining room.

"Yes?"

"My Lord, Sir Edward Moreton has arrived to see you. I have shown him into the library – "

"Ask cook to keep my chops warm, will you?" he replied, wiping his fat, red mouth and throwing down his napkin.

He rose from the table leaving Novella and her mother alone.

"Darling, you really should not vex your stepfather

so," admonished the Countess, as soon as the door was closed, "he has such a temper on him."

"Mama, I am so worried about you."

"It is nothing, as I have already told you. Just a silly, little cough."

"Even so, I wish you would see Doctor Jones."

"We cannot afford him at the moment, Novella."

"Money. Money. Money. That is all that is talked about in this house. Mama, Papa left us more than enough for ourselves and the upkeep of the house – I do not understand where it has all gone. Does he often ask for money from you?"

To her surprise, her mother began to cry.

"Darling, you do not understand," she snuffled, "he has rather high outgoings. I confess I did not realise the extent of his profligacy with money until after we had married. You must remember, he presented himself to me as a man of independent means – "

"But he must have his own money – he sold his estate."

"It all went on gambling debts and death duties. He has so many creditors, Novella, I dread the doorbell ringing. Why, only last month, I had to hand over my emeralds to bailiffs – can you imagine the shame? The *bailiffs,* calling at Crownley Hall!"

Novella stood up and ran to her mother, putting her arms around her.

"Novella, I fear I have been a foolish, old woman! It was just that I was so lonely after your Papa died and Lord Buckton seemed so kind and considerate. In truth, the moment we stepped out of the Church door, he turned into the man you now behold."

"But Papa's money – surely it is not all gone?"

"All but," confessed the Countess, "Novella, you must be strong for we stand on the brink of ruin."

"But it cannot be! I will do something, anything, to prevent it."

"I fear it may be too late."

With that, the Countess began to sob and then her sobs turned into a wracking cough. So long and hard did she cough, that her face turned red and her eyes began to stream.

"Mama, I will get help. Try and breathe slowly."

Novella ran to the servants' bell and pulled it hard and unceasingly.

In a flash, Mrs. Armitage was at the door, looking flustered.

"Help me get Mama upstairs to her room."

"Shall I send the stable lad to fetch the doctor, my Lady," asked Mrs. Armitage as they put the Countess to bed.

"Let us see how she is by the morning. I will go now and find my stepfather," said Novella, moving towards the door, "he should know that Mama is unwell."

It did not take Novella long to run to the library. The door was ajar as she reached it, so she knocked before entering.

"Lord Buckton, I am sorry to interrupt, but Mama has been taken ill!"

It was then that Novella looked at the other gentleman who sat in the room.

She tried not to show surprise on her face for rather than the portly, elderly gentleman she supposed Sir Edward Moreton to be, there sat a young, handsome man with a fine figure and noble features.

"I – I am sorry," she stammered, quite overwhelmed by Sir Edward's good looks.

"Ah, just the young lady I was hoping to see," he

replied, rising and bowing low. "I realise that this is not the best timing, naturally, but I feel that you would wish to have this returned to you."

He bent down to pick up something from beside him on the sofa.

"My bag! Where did it come from?" cried Novella, taking it from him.

"Constable Tompkins is a friend of mine and when I informed him that I was visiting the Hall, he bade me give this to the charming young lady whom he had the honour of driving home a few days before. Apparently, it was found by the woman who cleans the waiting room at the station."

Sir Edward bowed again and Novella noticed that he had a merry twinkle in his eye. Try as she might to dislike him, she immediately felt drawn to him. There was something about his warmth that was quite engaging.

"Thank you, sir, I am most grateful," she began.

"Now, run along, Novella, I have much to discuss with Sir Edward," interrupted Lord Buckton.

"But, sir, your wife is ill."

"And I will see to her once I have concluded my business with Sir Edward. Tending the sick is women's work – I will come when I am good and ready. Now, please leave us."

Novella felt sick inside. What kind of man was this who put his own interests before the welfare of his wife?

'Papa would have walked miles barefoot over red-hot coals to be with Mama, had she been taken ill!' thought Novella angrily as she mounted the stairs.

As she ascended, her thoughts turned to Sir Edward.

'I did not expect him to be so young,' she wondered, 'but I must not forget that he is the man who is at least partially responsible for not having Salamander at Crownley Hall."

Entering her mother's bedroom, Mrs. Armitage looked up, hopefully,

"His Lordship, is he with you? Her Ladyship has been asking for him."

"He is busy, Mrs. Armitage, and says he will come presently."

"Tch!"

Novella ignored the servant's cluck of disapproval. How could she say anything when she was in complete agreement with her? It was, indeed, a sorry state of affairs.

"Have you sent for the maid?"

"Yes, my Lady, she has gone downstairs to mix up an embrocation. My own dear mother gave me a recipe for one that I swear by."

"Thank you, Mrs. Armitage, I appreciate that."

Novella sank down on the Countess's bed and took her hand. Her face was pale and her lips had a slightly bluish tinge that Novella knew did not bode well.

"Mama, I am here," she whispered, as the Countess groaned softly.

"George, where is George?" she moaned.

"My Lady?" said Mrs. Armitage, quite puzzled.

"She is asking for Papa. Mama, Papa is dead."

"Oh! Oh!" cried the Countess.

"Shall I fetch his Lordship?" asked Mrs. Armitage, quite clearly unsure of what to do next.

"No, he is busy and will not come. Stay with Mama and I shall go and hurry up that maid."

Novella kissed her mother on the cheek and then left. As she descended the stairs, she cast a murderous look in the direction of the library. Reaching the hall, she saw that the maid was scurrying towards her with a jar covered with a cloth.

"Tell Mrs. Armitage that I am in the drawing room if she needs me when she has finished applying the embrocation."

"Very good, my Lady,"

The maid bobbed a quick curtsy and then ran up the stairs as fast as she could manage.

Inside the drawing room it was so cold that Novella shivered. The moon hung high and bright in the big picture window and illuminated the drive.

Novella sat down on a chair in the window, her thoughts whirling.

'What kind of man is this Lord Buckton?' she reflected, becoming angrier by the second. 'He shows no interest in Mama's health and talks endlessly about money. I do not like the fact that he has already frittered away all of his own money and, it would seem, he has also managed to plough through most of Mama's. What would Papa say? This is not what he would have wanted for her – no matter how lonely she was. Oh, Papa! Help us if you can! I fear for the very future of us all and that of Crownley Hall.'

She began to cry softly. It was not long before the moon became a blur and, in spite of herself, her eyes began to close, utterly exhausted by the evening's events.

CHAPTER THREE

The next day dawned and still Novella was most concerned about her mother's condition. Creeping into her bedroom as soon as she awoke, Novella found her coughing a great deal.

Mrs. Armitage was already by the Countess's side, with a cup of tea for her.

"She is no better, my Lady," she whispered, as Novella's mother struggled to sit up and take a sip of her tea.

"We should send for the doctor at once," replied Novella, wringing her hands.

"But his Lordship – he has said not to unless – "

"I do not care what his Lordship says, send the stable lad to fetch the doctor at once. He can take Folly – she is the swiftest horse we have."

"Very good, my Lady."

"And Mrs. Armitage – if his Lordship queries it, tell him that I will settle Doctor Jones's account myself."

"Yes, my Lady."

Novella picked up the cup and held it to her mother's lips.

"Come, Mama, try and drink this, it will soothe your chest."

"Thank you, darling, I confess I feel somewhat weak this morning."

"Do not fret, Mama – Mrs. Armitage is sending for Doctor Jones."

"Oh, I do not wish to bother him – "

"I insist, Mama. We must find out what is causing this cough."

Just then, Mrs. Armitage returned to the bedroom.

"Has the boy been sent?"

"Yes, my Lady. Shall I take over?"

"Thank you, Mrs. Armitage. Mama, I will return when the doctor has arrived. Please try and rest until then."

But the Countess was already asleep on the pillow, her mouth open, straining for breath.

'This is not right,' thought Novella, as she descended the stairs. She briefly visited the dining room to take some cold toast and then decided to proceed to her father's old study.

It was with bated breath that she opened the door – but sure enough, it was still as it had been on the day he died – with one exception.

'Where is the painting of the hunt at Thaxby?' questioned Novella for a second, before coming to the conclusion that it too had been a casualty of her stepfather's greed.

He had however shown a rare sensitivity in choosing not to occupy the study for his own. It was one of the smallest rooms in the house and did not afford a pleasant view out of the only window. Novella supposed that would have had something to do with it.

'Oh!' she cried, tears springing unbidden into her eyes, 'apart from the absence of the painting, it is as if he had just stepped away from his chair.'

Novella stroked the polished wood of his Moroccan leather-topped desk. The maid still came in here to clean so there was barely a speck of dust to be found.

'I remember Papa sitting at this desk, working away until Mama begged him to put down his pen.'

Her father had been a keen writer as well as managing the estates. A slim volume of his poetry had been published and he had written a few songs.

'I shall never meet a more talented man,' thought Novella. She also privately felt she would never love another as much as she had her father.

'I wonder what else my stepfather has seen fit to sell?' thought Novella, as she looked around the room. Then, it occurred to her that she should look in the drawers of the desk.

'I seem to recall that Papa kept some of his valuables here.'

She felt quite uncomfortable searching the drawers – it still felt like an intrusion of privacy. Novella found a gold pocket watch stuffed right at the back of the first drawer she opened, so she tucked it into the waistband of her skirt.

'I will keep this safe for Mama when she is well again,' she mused.

The next drawer was full of papers and little more of interest, but when she pulled open the bottom drawer, she was stunned to find, right on the very top of yet more papers, an envelope addressed to her.

'It is in Papa's hand!' she cried, her hands shaking.

For long moments, she simply sat and stared at it.

With a beating heart, she picked up her father's brass letter opener – the one with the owl on the top of it – and slid the blade underneath the seal.

Spreading out the sheet of paper flat so that she could read it, she found herself overcome with emotion at seeing that familiar hand once more.

The letter read,

"*My dearest daughter,*

I am no longer a young man, and even though I have not reached my three-score years and ten by a good mark, it is right that I make some provision for you should I die suddenly. My thoughts have been turning to my demise more frequently as I approach the age that my own dear father was taken from us."

'Goodness!' gasped Novella, 'I had quite forgotten that both Papa and Grandpapa died at the same age.'

She continued to read,

"*As I love you and your Mama more than you can ever know, and I love Crownley Hall almost as much, I have made sure that your futures will be secure. As you will both be ladies of considerable financial means upon my death, you will naturally become attractive to certain unsavoury elements – men who would court you only for your wealth.*

Much as I would hope that neither of you will fall prey to those with unscrupulous intent, I have decided to put aside a large portion of money that is held in trust by my dear friend and banker of many years – Mr. Hubert Longridge of the National Bank in Stockington.

If you are reading this, then I am gone and you must, in all haste, go to see him to stake your claim.

Only you or your mother can access these funds and Mr. Longridge has, in his possession, a legal document that states quite clearly that this account is free of the usual marital claim by a husband when a woman weds.

My darling, even if you have now spent all the money that was left to you in my original will, there is more where that came from.

The money will be made available to you on two conditions – that you will continue the upkeep of Crownley

Hall and that you will NEVER sell it. It is for your children and in turn, theirs.

Darling, I kiss you fervently from beyond the grave – I will always watch over you, no matter what.

Your affectionate father

George Crownley, Fifth Earl."

'Oh, Papa!' cried Novella, wiping away the tears and kissing the signature repeatedly, 'I miss you so much and we need your strength now more than ever.'

But tears soon gave way to elation as Novella realised that at last she possessed a way of safeguarding herself, her mother and the Hall from the excesses of Lord Buckton.

'I shall return the Hall to its former glory,' she said to herself, 'no matter what the expense. And now, I shall write to Mr. Longridge and request an appointment with him at his earliest convenience.'

Novella was just about to pull out a clean sheet of paper and begin to write when there came a soft knock at the door. Hastily, she hid her father's letter up her sleeve and bid whomever stood there to enter.

It was Mrs. Armitage – even so, she did not trust her not to go telling tales to Lord Buckton. Novella felt sure that the fact that she was found in her father's old study would go flying back to him.

"My Lady, Doctor Jones has just arrived."

"Thank you, Mrs. Armitage, I will come at once."

Novella shut the drawers of the desk and rose as calmly as she could.

"Ah, Lady Novella!" said Doctor Jones, as she entered her mother's room, "how lovely to see you again. It is a shame it is not in happier circumstances."

"How is Mama?"

"I feel we should go outside for a discussion," replied the doctor in an undertone.

He took Novella by the arm and led her outside.

"It is not good news?"

"I shall not lie to you, Lady Novella, for your mother is a very sick woman. I am afraid I cannot tell you what ails her exactly, for it is beyond my scope, but I would urge you to engage a specialist in these matters."

"But, surely you must have some notion of what her sickness can be?"

"I cannot be certain – it appears to be some kind of weakness in the chest. But Doctor von Haydn will be able to diagnose it more accurately. Here is his address. I fear he is not cheap, however, but I am sure that Lord Buckton will not shrink from the cost."

Novella paused for a second – she did not feel it was right to air her true feelings about her new stepfather with the doctor, even though he was an old family friend. It would not do for gossip about the state of their finances to reach the village.

"The cost will not be an issue, I can assure you," she replied, "now, will you take refreshment before you leave?"

The doctor put his hat on with a flourish and picked up his bag.

"I am afraid I do not have time – I have to visit Farmer Compton now, as his wife is also sick."

"Perhaps Mama has caught some kind of fever?" asked Novella, probing for a reason for her mother's sudden decline.

"I could not say, Lady Novella, now, if you will excuse me, I must be on my way. Is my carriage ready?"

"It is, doctor," replied Mrs. Armitage. "Ned is standing with your horse as you left him."

Novella and the doctor walked downstairs in silence.

She could tell that he was highly concerned about her mother, but she did not want to press him further.

She felt an awful presentiment of doom that she was trying hard to ignore.

As she watched the doctor drive off, Novella returned to her father's study.

Pulling out a clean sheet of paper from the pile on the desk, she began to write again to Mr. Hubert Longridge, asking to see him urgently.

'There,' she sighed, with a satisfied air as she addressed the letter. 'Now, I shall drive to the Post Office myself – I do not trust Mrs. Armitage or that stupid maid with such a precious missive.'

Pulling on a light wrap, as the day was warm, Novella ran to the stables and entreated Charles to make her buggy ready.

"Shall you be taking Folly out again, my Lady?" asked Charles, as Ned dragged the buggy into the yard. "Perhaps Bluebell would like a canter into the village."

"Bluebell will suit me very well," replied Novella, "and you are right, she will have precious little exercise whilst Mama is unwell."

"I see the doctor called this mornin', my Lady."

"Yes, Charles, but now we are forced to call in a specialist who studies diseases of the chest."

"His Lordship will not like the expense," warned Charles, a cross look on his face.

"I shall take care of it, Charles, and any other expense that is necessary."

Novella waited patiently whilst Bluebell was led out of her stall and tethered to the buggy. She sighed as she remembered Flash and Jock, the two fine stallions who used to pull the Crownley family carriages.

'I have yet to make my feelings known to Sir Edward,' she thought, recalling his handsome profile and charming smile. 'Once I have seen Mr. Longridge, then I shall pay him a visit too.'

For some inexplicable reason, Novella found herself rather looking forward to that day.

She was soon on her way up the drive. It had been some time since the buggy had been used and it was dusty and in need of repair. Novella thought that it would not look too good to be seen in the village in such a poor contraption, but she had no choice.

Her stepfather, as usual, had taken the only decent carriage to London and she would have to put up with the buggy.

Even so, as she drew into the main street, she could feel the eyes of the villagers upon her. A few waved in recognition, but there were also some who avoided her gaze.

'No matter,' she thought, as she pulled Bluebell up outside the Post Office. 'I shall be glad of some friendly discourse with Mrs. Cruickshank – she is always so full of news.'

The Post Office was also the general store and sold all manner of tinned and dried goods. It smelled of tea and brown paper – Novella had often visited it when she was a child and had not been inside for some two and a half years.

"My Lady! What brings you to the village. I did not realise that you were back at the Hall."

Mrs. Cruickshank was tall and thin but with a friendly face. Her steel-grey hair was pulled back in a tight bun and she wore a blue shawl over her navy cotton dress. For an elderly lady of sixty years, she was very sprightly.

"It is good to see you again."

"And how is your dear Mama? We do not hear much of the Countess since she married – *him*."

Novella ignored the barely concealed distaste that the old Postmistress displayed, but it gave her some satisfaction even so, knowing that she was not alone in her dislike of Lord Buckton.

"She is a little unwell, I am sorry to say. We were forced to send for Doctor Jones only this morning."

"It will be the damp. Your Mama is too much of a lady to withstand this wet weather we've been having lately. But today is lovely, I am glad to say. Now, what can I do for you?"

"I wish this letter to be sent to Stockington immediately."

Novella handed her the letter destined for Mr. Longridge.

"Ah, I have a parcel to be delivered to that very same gentleman and that too is urgent. It will leave here almost before you have climbed back into your buggy."

"Mrs. Cruickshank, tell me some news. I have been starved of it whilst I was cloistered away at the girls' school."

Mrs. Cruickshank positively beamed – if there was one thing she loved, it was a long chat on who was doing what in the village.

"Will you take some tea? I can close up for just half an hour?"

Novella nodded, smiling to herself all the while.

'I do believe I have made Mrs. Cruickshank's day,' she thought, as the old lady ushered her to a chair by the counter.

It was not long before she heard the kettle whistling in the back room. It made Novella feel really comfortable – she missed the fact that she could no longer run down into the kitchen and gossip with cook. She did not in the least like the look of Higgins, the new cook.

She felt certain that she would be in league with Mrs.

Armitage, and she still did not trust her not to report back her every action and utterance to her and then to Lord Buckton.

With her mother so ill, it made Novella feel so alone and in need of company.

"Here you are, my Lady."

Mrs. Cruickshank bustled through from the back room carrying a tray laden with tea and biscuits.

"Let me help you," offered Novella, rising to her feet.

"No, no, my Lady. There, it is all done."

She began to pour the tea and then proffered the cup – Novella noticed that it was barely used bone china – probably Mrs. Cruickshank's best.

"Now, where shall I begin?"

"Tell me everything, Mrs. Cruickshank, I want to hear every last piece of news."

"Well, Mrs. Carburton has had twins, a boy and a girl and old Farmer Pete has packed up and left to live by the sea. Can you imagine such a thing? 'You won't find many pigs in Brighton,' I told him."

"And what of the servants who used to work at Crownley Hall?"

Mrs. Cruickshank looked down at her boots and coughed.

"I am not sure I should say, my Lady. It was a terrible business, what happened when Lord Buckton came to Crownley Hall – "

The old lady hesitated and cast a worried glance at Novella.

"Do go on, Mrs. Cruickshank, I shall not be offended. Please, say what is on your mind."

"Well, my Lady, we were all so shocked. Some of the servants had been under his Lordship, the Earl, since they were young ones. And, as for Wargrave, he started out as a footman to your father when he was just a boy."

"Tell me what happened, Mrs. Cruickshank."

Novella reached forward and squeezed the old lady's hand.

"I want to know *everything*."

Mrs. Cruickshank looked once over her shoulder and then leaned forward so that she was nearer to Novella.

"It all happened one morning, my Lady. Lord Buckton had not been in the house five minutes afore he was throwing his weight around – ordering things to be taken down and sold off. And then there was that dreadful business with the Tower. Lord! What an omen for a marriage."

Mrs. Cruickshank crossed herself as if to protect herself from further harm.

"I hear tell that her Ladyship, the Countess, was distraught. Wanted to go away for a long holiday, but Lord Buckton would not. And then he goes and decides that they don't need so many servants – too costly, he said.

"In the space of two hours, my Lady, Wargrave, Sally, Gerald and Harry were all sent packing without any notice. When Wargrave tried to protest, he had his reference ripped up right in front of his eyes by Lord Buckton."

"But, he would not be able to find another position without a reference. That is shocking!" cried Novella, almost dropping her teacup. "What has happened to him?"

"Last I heard he had gone to live with his sister in Chichester – but he's a broken man, my Lady, you mark my words."

There was a long silence as the two women finished their tea.

Novella felt an incredible sadness upon hearing about the way their faithful servants had been treated. Her father would have been outraged.

And what of her stepfather? Novella knew that newcomers were always viewed with suspicion until they proved themselves worthy, and she was anxious to know what kind of impression Lord Buckton had created in the village – but did she dare ask?

As if she had read her mind, Mrs. Cruickshank took a deep breath and said,

"My Lady, can I speak my mind?"

"Mrs. Cruickshank, I have already said that you may, so pray, continue."

"It is just that I worry for you and your dear mother. The Countess is a good lady and does not deserve the lack of respect that this man has shown her."

"You can rest assured that whatever you say will not go further than these walls."

"My Lady, there is talk in the village that Lord Buckton visits a lady – if you understand my meaning – when he goes to London. I would not tell you but for the sake of the Countess – we still all love her in the village."

"I had guessed as much," replied Novella, quietly.

"My Lady, I do not wish to upset you – " said the old lady, dabbing at her eyes.

"Be still, Mrs. Cruickshank, I thank you for your honesty with me. Now, I must take my leave as I have much to do. How much do I owe you for the postage?"

"Nothing, my Lady. Just promise me that you will save the Countess and Crownley Hall from destruction!"

Novella hugged her close saying,

"There is one more thing I would ask of you."

"Anything, my Lady, you just name it."

"I wish to find Sally, my old maid. Do you know where I might find her?"

Mrs. Cruickshank quickly walked to the counter and took up a pencil and a piece of card.

She scribbled down an address and handed it to Novella.

"Here, my Lady. Tell her that I gave it to you with my best wishes."

"*Willow Cottage, Bell Lane.* Is that not the cottage that the old school teacher lived in until she died?"

"Yes, my Lady."

"But I had thought that it had been knocked down."

"It is Sally's address, of that I am certain."

"Thank you, Mrs. Cruickshank, goodbye, I hope I see you again soon."

"You will, my Lady, you will."

And with that, Novella found herself back out on the street. She untethered Bluebell and clambered back into the buggy.

Flicking the reins, Bluebell started off down the road towards the edge of the village.

'I hope that Sally is at home,' thought Novella as they approached the top of Bell Lane.

She was travelling for some time before the cottage came into view.

Stopping outside, Novella was dismayed to see that it was even more run down than she remembered it. One of the front windows was broken and boarded up roughly with planks of wood and the garden path was so overgrown that she was forced to beat her way to the front door.

'Surely Sally cannot be living here,' she murmured, rapping hard on the door, for the knocker had long since disappeared.

But sure enough, the head that peeped out from behind the door was that of her old maid.

"My Lady! You are back. Praise the Heavens!"

Sally flung the door wide open and grabbed both of Novella's hands, warmly.

"Yes, Sally, I am back."

"You will come in, of course?" invited Sally, pulling her over the threshold.

Inside, the room was as homely as it could be given that the wallpaper was peeling off the walls and threadbare curtains hung at the broken window.

"You will excuse the mess, my Lady," said Sally, bobbing a curtsy.

"Sally, you no longer have to curtsy to me."

"It does not seem right, my Lady, but I am so glad, so very glad, that you have returned to Crownley Hall. Oh, it vexes me so – the devilry that has been going on there. His Lordship, the Earl, must be spinning in his grave like a top!"

"Sally?"

The girl bowed her head,

"My Lady, it is not for me to say – "

Novella grabbed the girl's hand and stared straight into her eyes. There were tears there that were threatening to spill down her once lovely cheeks.

"I implore you, Sally, you must tell me."

Sally took a deep breath and then spoke urgently, her bottom lip trembling all the while.

"My Lady, you and her Ladyship are in terrible danger – I would not say this if I did not know that it were true. My Lady," she said, pausing dramatically, "there is something I need to tell you – "

And with that, she rose to close the curtains before beginning her tale.

CHAPTER FOUR

An hour later, Novella left Sally's cottage, her mind reeling. What Sally had told her had both shocked and appalled her.

Even though she had suspected that her new stepfather was a little unscrupulous, and, in the light of what Mrs. Cruickshank had told her, immoral, but she now also believed him to be utterly evil.

She had not wanted to believe what the trembling, former servant had told her – the conversation that she had overheard when she was cleaning the fender in the library and crouched behind a chair – the strange men who were shown around the Hall who seemed to be taking measurements.

"I tell you, my Lady, he was up to no good!" Sally had said fiercely.

And as Novella digested the information, she too came to the same conclusion.

She recalled Sally's pale face as she had recounted her stepfather's words to one of his friends,

"My Lady, without a word of a lie, this is what I heard. I would swear on my mother's grave! Lord Buckton told his friend that as soon as he had 'dealt with the problem of her Ladyship' he intended to sell Crownley Hall to a Bradford millionaire who would probably knock it down to build a new house. He said nothing would stop him and if he had to help fate along, then he would!"

"Surely, he could not mean – " Novella had asked, not wishing to utter the word 'murder'.

"My Lady, he had such a temper on him, I would not put it past him. Nearly beat one of the stable boys to within in inch of his life, he did! I never saw a man so out of control. It were only Charles pulling the boy away that saved him. Her Ladyship paid the boy's doctor's bills in secret, God bless her."

Novella had listened to Sally with ever-growing horror. Sally was right, both she and the Countess were in danger. But how could she prove anything? A servant's hearsay counted for naught.

'I will relay my fears to Mr. Longridge – he will guide me,' she said to herself as she climbed at last back onto the buggy.

Novella resolved to send Sally some money, once she had visited the bank.

'The poor girl – she seems so ground down by what has happened to her. I cannot think how she ekes out a living. My stepfather must have believed himself the most fortunate of men – having a wealthy, lonely widow with a massive property at his disposal. It fair makes my blood boil!'

As she drove along, snippets of Sally's story kept coming back to her – how Lord Buckton had steadfastly stayed by her mother's side after her father had died and how he told her not to bother her head with anything odious as he would take care of it.

'He is a sly one,' concluded Novella, becoming angrier at each mile. 'And to think he also keeps a mistress in London! I had guessed as much. The man is totally without shame or scruples. Mama should be rid of him as soon as she can.'

But in her heart, Novella knew that this was unlikely to happen. Her mother was not strong and she had always relied upon men to tell her what to do and when. Novella was so unlike her – and it was all thanks to her father who had brought her up to be strong and independent.

'Papa was a rare man,' mused Novella, as she pulled into the drive of the Hall. 'Yet for all his encouragement, Mama let him rule the roost without question. It has certainly been her undoing.'

*

Novella could only count the hours until she received a reply to her letter from Mr. Longridge. She guessed that she should not expect an immediate response, as he would inevitably be a very busy man.

'I must be patient,' she reminded herself, as she paced up and down her father's study.

She brooded upon all she had seen and heard that day for quite some time.

She hid in her father's study, preferring solitude.

Every hour or so, she would go up to her mother's bedroom and check on her. There had been a slight change – her breathing was not so laboured and she was sitting up in bed, saying that she might get up for dinner. However, she was still experiencing the most intense chest pains.

'Mama needs constant nursing and it is unfair to expect Mrs. Armitage to undertake those duties,' thought Novella, returning to the study once more.

'I will look into engaging a nurse. I am certain that Mama will improve with continual care.'

She stayed in the study until quite late. She was just about to leave the room when she heard noises in the hallway – it was her stepfather returning from London.

'No doubt refreshed from visiting his lady friend,

whilst his poor wife lies ill upstairs,' thought Novella, murderously.

She waited until she heard his footsteps dying away up the stairs before she emerged and then she quickly made her way to her own room.

With a resigned sigh, Novella began to dress for dinner. She wondered if her mother would appear at table and secretly hoped that she would. She hated the idea of having to dine alone with her stepfather.

Eventually, the huge gong in the downstairs hallway sounded, so Novella braced herself and quietly left her room.

'I must try not to argue with stepfather,' she repeated to herself as she entered the dining room.

However she was the first down for the room was empty.

Mrs. Armitage was nowhere to be seen, but Lily, the maid, was standing there ready to serve the meal.

"Good evening!" came a booming voice behind her.

Novella turned around to see Lord Buckton standing there, a supercilious smile playing around his lips. He fingered the end of his moustache and gave Novella a withering look.

"Good evening," murmured Novella, sitting down with her back to him. "How did you find London?"

"Hectic, as always. Dirty and noisy. I swear I could not live there in its foul air for any amount of money."

"Quite," replied Novella, with just the merest hint of sarcasm in her voice.

"But London has its advantages and many distractions," he continued, gesturing to the maid to fill his glass.

"I would expect it does," she countered, feigning interest in the napkin in front of her.

Novella sat waiting for him to enquire after the health of her mother – but instead, he chattered on about a play he had seen that afternoon at a matinee.

She was just about to make a remark when the dining room door opened and there, looking pale and frail, stood her mother.

"Mama!" she cried, rising from the table.

"Don't get up, dear, I can manage," replied the Countess, making her way slowly to her chair.

"How are you feeling, Mama?"

"A little better, thank you."

There was still no sound except that of Lord Buckton tapping his ring absent-mindedly against his plate.

"Anthony?" said the Countess, by way of greeting.

"Oh, yes – er – you are well?"

"Not quite, sir, but I was so bored lying upstairs that I longed for a change of scenery."

"Is that wise, Mama. Would not your bed be better for you?"

"Hush, Novella, dear. I want to be here."

The maid brought the first course – some cold lobster – and the three of them ate in silence.

"Doctor Jones came this morning," began Novella.

"That old quack. I hope he did not charge you more than a guinea for the privilege," countered Lord Buckton.

Novella continued,

"I met his costs out of my own pocket, sir, so you have no need to fret on that account. However, I am afraid that he was unable to determine what ails Mama, and so he has recommended that she see a specialist in chest complaints. His name is Doctor von Haydn and he is from London."

"And will cost a pretty penny, no doubt. No, it is out

of the question. You are feeling better, are you not, madam?"

Novella looked at her mother's pale face that was breaking out in small beads of perspiration at the effort she was making to be present. It was pitiful and Novella's tender heart surged out to her.

"I – I am not terribly well, I must confess," replied the Countess.

"Stuff and nonsense! Fresh air and beef tea is all you need. And Mrs. Armitage's embrocation."

Novella could not help herself but she had to intervene.

"Doctor Jones thought it more serious than that, sir. I intend to write to Doctor von Haydn and ask him to call at the Hall to see Mama. I will not rest easy until I am assured that what ails her is not serious."

"And I say it is not. Your Mama has a weak constitution and as such is prone to lingering maladies and fantasies that she is seriously ill. No, such a waste of money is out of the question. Let that be the last word on it."

Novella bit her lip and said no more.

'I do not care what he says, I will pay for Doctor von Haydn to visit Mama,' she thought.

Her stepfather was so often away from the Hall that by the time he found out that he had called, the specialist would have been and gone.

"Whilst we are on the subject of money," began Lord Buckton, as the main course arrived. "I wish to discuss the matter of that dreadful carriage."

He picked up a bone from his plate and began to strip it of meat.

'How very apt,' thought Novella, as she watched him. His awful table manners almost put her off her own meal.

"What about the carriage?" asked the Countess fearfully.

"It will not do for a gentleman of my standing to be seen in such a derelict object. When I am in London, I should have a smarter vehicle to take me around."

"But, sir, the expense – " she replied, meekly.

"Silence," he roared, "specialists we do not need, but I have a reputation to keep up. I should like you to release some funds so that I may purchase a new carriage."

"But – but, I do not have any more money, Anthony, dear. You took the last hundred pounds I had to pay your tailor."

Lord Buckton glared at her, masticating malevolently on a piece of partridge and then tearing some more meat from a wing as he snarled,

"So you wish me to look like a tramp on the road, do you?"

"No, but – "

"What is there left that we can sell from this stinking heap of bricks?" he said, his tone tart and uncompromising.

Novella wanted to jump in and say something, but her mother shot her a warning glance.

"There is very little, sir."

"Then I will have to sell some of those baubles that you never wear. That pearl necklace for instance."

"But that was a wedding present from you!" cried the Countess, her chest heaving with distress.

"I gave it to you, so it is mine to sell should I wish. We will say no more and you will kindly hand it over after dinner, madam,"

Novella watched helplessly as her mother began to cry softly. Then the tears became a cough that would not cease.

Rushing to her mother's side, Novella quickly rang for Mrs. Armitage.

Her stepfather ignored the scene unfolding in front of

him and simply continued eating.

"There, there, Mama. Do not distress yourself, try and breathe deeply, it will help you."

"I should go back to bed," she answered, and almost immediately was gripped by another coughing fit.

"You shall, at once, Mama. Ah, here is Mrs. Armitage."

The two women helped the Countess from the table as she coughed piteously.

Casting a backward glance at her impervious stepfather, Novella was filled with loathing.

"No matter what he says, I will summon Doctor van Haydn, Mama," she whispered, as they made their way upstairs.

As soon as her mother was in bed, Novella sent Mrs. Armitage to the kitchen for some hot water, lemon and honey.

She kissed her mother on the forehead and smoothed back her hair.

"I shall retire now, but have Mrs. Armitage wake me if you need me."

"Yes, darling," murmured her mother, drowsily.

'I do hope that Mr. Longridge makes haste with his reply,' thought Novella as she moved towards her own room. 'Mama is seriously ill, no matter what my stepfather believes.'

*

Thankfully, Novella did not have to wait long, for bright and early the next morning, the postman arrived bearing a reply from Mr. Longridge.

She tried not to look too excited as Mrs. Armitage handed it to her at the breakfast table – she did not wish to arouse her stepfather's curiosity.

She returned to her room and, locking the door behind her, opened the letter.

"Thank Heavens!" she cried as she read the elegant script,

"My dear Novella,

How glad I am to hear that you are back where you belong – at Crownley Hall. I have long been concerned for the welfare of your mother since her most recent marriage and we have much to discuss.

Pray be at my office this afternoon at 2.30pm at the National Bank in Stockington.

Yours truly,

Hubert Longridge."

'At last, I will be able to find out what was so important that Papa hid a letter in his desk for me,' she thought, as she made her way downstairs.

Her heart was so much lighter as she ran towards the stables – both in anticipation of seeing the horses, but also because she felt that at last, she had found a way to safeguard her and her mother's interests.

As she approached the stables, she could hear an unfamiliar voice talking to Charles, the groom. Rounding the corner, she saw that it was the handsome man who had brought back her bag.

"Sir Edward," she said, somewhat icily, "what brings you to Crownley Hall? There are no more horses to be found for sale here – you have already bought our best."

Sir Edward bowed with a mischievous smile playing about his lips,

"Lady Novella, how delightful to see you."

The way he said it made Novella blush. There was something in his tone that made her feel awkward and nervous.

"My stepfather is out so I am afraid that you have made a wasted journey," she replied, tartly.

"I have come to collect a few saddles that Lord Buckton promised me. I was not able to take them with me the last time we met as I was on horseback and not in my carriage."

Novella could not resist it, but there was one question she longed to ask him,

"How is Salamander?"

Sir Edward laughed merrily, his eyes twinkling,

"He is settling in very well, Lady Novella. You must come very soon and see for yourself. I am sure that he misses you as much as you do him. I should be glad to show you around my house – it is not as grand as Crownley Hall, but you will find it most comfortable."

Novella was bursting to reply in the affirmative, but she held back. She had been wrong-footed by Sir Edward's charm and friendliness, but all her frostiness was dissolving in the face of his brilliant smile.

"Thank you very much, I should enjoy that."

"Shall we say, Wednesday?" asked Sir Edward eagerly.

Novella had the distinct feeling that he had an ulterior motive in inviting her to his home, but she did not care to ponder it too closely.

"I shall have to consult my diary – if I could write and let you know?" she answered, almost unable to conceal her joy at the prospect of riding her beloved Salamander once again.

Sir Edward bowed and gave her another charming smile.

To her consternation, Novella was feeling increasingly disarmed by him.

But just then, Charles came struggling out of the stable bearing her best saddle.

"That be the last one, Sir Edward," he puffed, as he heaved the heavily tooled piece into the box on the rear of the carriage.

Novella did not say a word, but she could feel tears pricking at her eyes.

'And to think I believed him to be a decent man! He is full of nothing but fine words laced with the poison of deceit.'

She did not stop to say goodbye, but ran back towards the house.

"Lady Novella. Wait!" cried Sir Edward, obviously having seen her expression, "it is not as it appears – "

But his words were lost to her as she vanished out of sight.

*

Although Novella had already been in to see her mother more than once that morning, she paid her another visit after she had recovered from her encounter with Sir Edward.

Novella found her still weak and, if anything, set back by the previous night's sortie to the dining room.

"Mama, it was foolish of you to attempt to get up when you are not quite better," admonished Novella, as she gave her a drink of lemon-barley water.

"I do not wish to be any bother, Novella, dear. You must try to go about your normal routine without worrying about me."

"But I do, Mama. Come what may, we will send for Doctor van Haydn at once."

"But your stepfather – "

"Ssh, no more. Try and sleep. I shall return after

luncheon. I have an appointment in Stockington this afternoon."

Novella kissed her mother, trying not to show how worried she was. The Countess was deathly pale and drawn and seemed to be having difficulty in breathing.

Novella took luncheon in her room and then made herself ready for her appointment.

'I do hope that Lord Buckton has taken his horse,' she thought, as she walked towards the stables. For such an important visit, only the family carriage would do.

"Sorry, my Lady, Lord Buckton took the carriage this mornin'," explained Charles, as Novella sighed in exasperation. "You will have to take the buggy."

"I shall look like the poor relation instead of the daughter of an Earl!" she cried.

"Can't be helped, my Lady, but look, I gave Folly a right good going over and she looks a treat."

Ned brought Folly out, snorting and whinnying excitedly.

"See, my Lady, she's excited at seeing you."

'And I long to see Salamander,' thought Novella, casting her mind back to their visitor that morning. Even though she was still outraged that Sir Edward had bought her best saddle, her desire to see her beloved horse was stronger.

'I will write to him and accept his kind invitation,' determined Novella, as she climbed up onto the buggy. 'I shall have to swallow my distaste for the circumstances – I will do almost anything to mount Salamander again.'

It did not take Novella long before she was pulling into Stockington. But to her dismay, she could only progress very slowly as it was market day.

By the time she reached the bank, she was almost twenty minutes late. Novella quickly tied Folly up to the post and ran inside.

She need not have worried. Mr. Longridge welcomed her into his office with a beaming smile.

He was a small, round man with a friendly face and was in the habit of wearing brightly coloured waistcoats.

"I am so sorry that I am late," apologised Novella, quite red in the face – she hated not being punctual as she felt that lateness was the height of bad manners.

"Come, come, my dear, you are here and that is all that matters. Would you care for some tea? I can ask Thomas to bring some in."

"Thank you," replied Novella, sinking down in the chair that Mr. Longridge had offered her.

"My dear, I cannot tell you how glad I am that you have come at last. I have waited too long for this day to dawn – too long!"

At that moment, there was a knock on the door and Thomas came in with two cups of tea.

"Leave us now and do not disturb us please."

Mr. Longridge shut the door behind his assistant and then squeezed behind his desk. Taking down a fat file from the shelf, he brushed it off before opening it.

"Now my dear, to business," he started. "We have much to discuss, Lady Novella. Much – your dear father was quite specific, quite specific. My Lady, you are about to become very rich indeed, but there are certain conditions – "

CHAPTER FIVE

Mr. Hubert Longridge listened to Novella as she told him all that had occurred at Crownley Hall since her return. He nodded and made sympathetic noises, occasionally shaking his head in disbelief at what she was recounting.

"I must confess," he said, smoothing out a document that he had taken from the file in front of him, "I had no clue where your father had hidden his letter to you. I was forced to simply wait until such time as you contacted me. Had you not been in touch – then, my dear, I do not know what I should have done."

"Until I found the letter, I had no idea that Papa had made extra provision for us. Sadly, my stepfather seems intent on draining Mama's coffers dry. To tell the truth, I live in fear of what might happen to us and Crownley Hall should he have his way."

Mr. Longridge rustled the papers again and coughed,

"Which is precisely why your father put in place these unusual arrangements. We often used to sit and discuss what might happen after his death and his worst fear was that the Hall would fall into another's hands and be sold off. From what you have told me, I have every reason to suspect that your stepfather does not have the best interests of the estate at heart."

"The place is in a terrible state of repair," explained Novella. "Did you know that there had been a fire in the

West wing and that the Tower had been struck by lightning? So, while the house falls down around our ears, Lord Buckton's only concern appears to be that the family carriage is not smart enough for his jaunts to London. Crownley Hall is not a priority for him in the least."

"Such an attitude was just what your father was afraid of. He was realistic about your Mama – he knew that she would be lost without a male presence in her life and he guessed that she might remarry, should she outlive him. The Earl trusted you very much, Novella, he knew that you loved the house and the horses as much as he did."

"Sadly, it is too late for the horses – all, except the old ones have been sold," sighed Novella with a heavy heart. "Lord Buckton was good enough not to sell Mama's mount, Bluebell, and another cross-bred mare called Folly, but the rest, including my Salamander, have gone to Sir Edward Moreton."

"Hmm, yes, I am acquainted with that gentleman. A very fine, upstanding young man he is too. You should have no worries about their welfare, they will be treated better than some humans."

Mr. Longridge attempted a smile, but upon seeing Novella's wan face, full of misery, he swiftly moved on to the business in hand.

"Now," he continued, "the Earl was very specific in this codicil to his main will. It says that in the event of your mother remarrying, or you marrying for the first time, then under no circumstances will either spouse, or subsequent spouses, be able to claim any rights to their wives' estates or the separate fund."

"So am I to understand that there is yet more money for us?"

"That is correct. A substantial amount it is too. It should be more than enough to take care of the repairs to

Crownley Hall that you mentioned and to keep you both very comfortable for a number of years. Your father knew that upon his death, such would be the wealth that you and your mother would inherit, that it would make you both very attractive to certain unsavoury elements. He wished to protect you both and the Hall. Listen to this paragraph – "

And with that, he began to read the long letter that accompanied the will. As he read, Novella's eyes filled with tears and she could not prevent herself from weeping.

'It is like having Papa in the room,' she said to herself, dabbing at her eyes.

As Mr. Longridge finished reading, Novella composed herself – there were so many questions she longed to ask.

"You said that there was one important condition upon which this will rests, Mr. Longridge. Pray, what might that be?"

"It is simple," replied Mr. Longridge, sitting back in his chair, "the only stipulation is that the Hall should never be sold during your lifetimes as if you did so, it would immediately nullify the will and your funds would become inaccessible."

"So, am I able to spend the money on a specialist for Mama?"

"Is she unwell?" enquired Mr. Longridge, a look of concern on his rounded features.

"I am afraid so. Doctor Jones could not say what ailed her, but advised that we should engage the services of a specialist from London. Needless to say, my stepfather forbade the expense."

"Outrageous!" exclaimed Mr. Longridge. "What kind of man refuses his wife the very best when she is ill?"

Novella tactfully did not comment. However, there was more one question she desperately needed to ask,

"And would the will allow me to buy back our horses, should Sir Edward be persuaded to part with them?"

"Naturally. Your father was not so draconian that he laid down strict rules about what you could and could not spend the money on. His only wish was that the Hall did not suffer. You must proceed with whatever plans you have for the Hall and for yourself. A nice, long holiday for you and the Countess once she has recovered, perhaps?"

Novella shook her head.

"I am not confident of a full recovery, Mr. Longridge. Mama has never been strong and I fear the worst. But it is good news that I will have the money to repair the Hall – I shall engage some workmen immediately as we need to have the works finished before the winter sets in."

"That is wise, indeed. The weather will do its worst if you allow things to remain as they are and then it will cost you three times as much."

Mr. Longridge rose and replaced the file on the shelf.

"I am at your disposal whenever you need me, my Lady. Please remember that. You now have no need to worry as your stepfather cannot get his hands on any of your money, that is, unless you choose to give it to him."

"Mama may well do so, Mr. Longridge, so I fear I may indulge in a little underhand deception until such time as I judge her to be free of Lord Buckton's influence."

"That day may not come, if what you have told me is true," he replied, before adding – "oh, and there is one other matter – there is one other person who knows about this part of your father's will – Mr. Humbert Senior of Rumbold and Humbert, the family's solicitors. Should you find yourself in any difficulties, you must ask for him and not his son or his partner."

"Thank you, I have taken up enough of your time already. I have lots of calls to make on my way back home."

"The stonemason and the builder, perhaps?"

"Precisely," agreed Novella, suddenly feeling rejuvenated at the prospect. "Thank you so very much, Mr. Longridge. I was beginning to feel quite alone but now I believe I have an ally at last."

"Remember, Lady Novella, your father was a dear friend of mine as well as a customer and it is no lie when I say that I extend the same compliment to you. You are not alone, my dear, not alone!"

Before she concluded her business, Novella requested that some money be withdrawn at once so that she could begin to renovate the Hall.

She also asked Mr. Longridge to send a messenger round with a five-pound note for Sally. Novella knew that if she tried to give it to her herself, she would only refuse to take it.

Novella left the bank feeling considerably happier than when she entered.

'I feel as if a load has been lifted from my shoulders,' she said to herself, as she stroked Folly's silky mane. 'First, we shall visit the stonemasons and then Gross, the family builders.'

*

It was past teatime when Novella eventually returned to Crownley Hall. As she pulled into the stables, she could see that the family carriage was back.

'That means that my stepfather is also at home,' she concluded, 'well, I have nothing to fear. He can say what he will, but words will not harm me.'

Knowing that she was protected financially gave Novella a new courage. She would stand up to her stepfather – *she would*!

Novella had barely set one foot inside the hallway when Lily, the maid, came rushing up to her.

"My Lady, Lord Buckton wishes to see you in the drawing room."

"Very well, I will proceed there at once," accepted Novella, anxious to have any ugly scenes over with as soon as possible.

"And where might you have been all afternoon, young lady?" he roared, as soon as she entered the room. It was obvious that Lord Buckton was in a foul humour.

"I had some business in Stockington," she replied coolly.

"And what might that be?" he spat.

Novella thought that she could smell drink on him, but even so, it did not cower her.

"What I was doing there is my business and mine alone."

"Not while you live under my roof."

"Sir, it is not your roof. The Hall belongs to Mama and me."

Lord Buckton hurtled towards her, but stopped short.

"I am your mother's husband and so, by default, it belongs to me. I repeat, what was your business?"

Novella steeled herself inwardly and then, with one eye on the door, replied,

"Sir, I repeat too that I am not answerable to you. *You are not my father*. Now, if you will excuse me, I am dishevelled from travelling in that open buggy and wish to change."

And with that, she stalked out of the room. Behind her, she could hear her stepfather's exhortations for her to return, but she bravely continued on her way up to her mother's room.

'I do hope Mama is awake,' thought Novella, 'I would doubt that Lord Buckton has been in to see her at all today.'

Opening the bedroom door, she could smell Mrs. Armitage's embrocation – the pungent scents of eucalyptus and camphor hung heavily in the air. Mrs. Armitage was seated next to the bed knitting.

"My Lady," she whispered, as Novella tiptoed inside, "she has only just gone to sleep, forgive me if I do not wake her."

"How is she?"

"Coughing terribly, my Lady."

"I shall write to Doctor von Haydn in the morning and see if he can come out to see Mama," stated Novella. "I shall also make enquiries about engaging the services of a nurse. You have done very well but I am certain that you have other duties that you need to catch up with."

"Well, I'm not sure what Lord Buckton will have to say about all that. It will cost a pretty penny. But you are very right, my Lady, that lazy girl Lily needs a good broom behind her. And I cannot do it being up here half the day. I did not bargain for nursing when I came to work at Crownley Hall. I am a housekeeper, not a nursemaid."

Rising from her chair, Mrs. Armitage left the room.

Novella sat next to her mother and watched her laboured breathing. It was heart-rending to see her so ill.

"Oh, Mama," she whispered, "please do your best to get well soon. I promise I will get all the help I can and it has been made possible by my own dear Papa. I found a letter in his desk, telling us that there was more money. But we must keep it a secret from everyone."

The Countess's eyes flickered for a moment and Novella started, thinking she was about to wake up – but she did not.

Novella sat there for as long as she could – she heard the dinner gong sound but stayed where she was. About an hour later, Lily brought her some cold meat and bread on a tray.

"Your stepfather was enquiring as to where you were, my Lady, but Mrs. Armitage told him that she was sick of nursing and that a proper nurse had to be engaged else she was going to walk out. He was furious but he could not say anything. I bet you're glad you weren't there to see it."

"Yes, I am, Lily. My stepfather is most ill-humoured this evening and I wanted to keep Mama company."

"I'll be leaving you then, my Lady. Will you be wanting any more supper?"

"No thank you, I shall be retiring shortly as I am quite exhausted myself."

After the maid had closed the door, Novella ate her meagre meal, then sat by her mother's bedside until sleep overtook her.

*

Novella remained thus, in the armchair, for the whole night and woke with a start when Lily came in at half-past six to clean the grate and relight the fire.

"Goodness," she yawned, stretching her arms and legs. "I am so stiff."

Rising from the armchair, Novella wandered downstairs. She did not wish to encounter her stepfather, so she slipped down the back stairs to the kitchen.

Mrs. Armitage was nowhere to be seen so Novella helped herself to a large slice of bread and butter. Wandering around, she found a tray of tea, ready to go up to the dining room.

'It will not matter if I take my tea here,' she thought, pouring out a cup.

As she stood in the kitchen with the morning light pouring in the back window, she could see the ruined Tower.

She smiled to herself as she thought of the extra

money her father had secreted away for her.

'Not much longer – soon you will look as magnificent as before,' she whispered, as if the Tower were alive and could hear her.

Finishing her bread and tea, she returned back upstairs.

'I should write the letter to Doctor von Haydn,' she told herself, walking towards her father's study.

She always felt a sense of relief as soon as she closed the door behind her, and allowed herself to be enveloped by the welcoming smell of books and leather.

Even though she felt tired and her bones ached from sitting in the chair all night, she had to pull herself together to write the letter.

It was only half written when there came a knock at the door.

"Who is it?" she called, hiding the half-written note in a drawer.

"It's Mrs. Armitage, my Lady."

Without waiting to be invited in, Mrs. Armitage pushed open the door and stood in front of Novella, a sour look on her face.

"There is a gentleman here to see you, my Lady – Sir Edward Moreton."

'Oh, Heavens!' thought Novella, catching sight of her reflection in a glass bookcase door. 'I do not have time to make myself presentable, Sir Edward will have to take me as he finds me.'

Walking towards the drawing room, Novella wondered what business could have brought him to the Hall. It was then that she remembered that she had said she would write and let him know if she would be visiting him the next day.

'It had quite gone out of my mind,' she thought, as she

hesitated outside the door.

As she entered the room, she suddenly felt quite awkward and wished that she had taken time to run upstairs and splash her face or maybe change her dress.

"Ah, Lady Novella. I trust I have not inconvenienced you by arriving at such an early hour."

'I must look a fright,' reckoned Novella, trying to avoid Sir Edward's intense gaze.

It was then, when she looked up at him, that she noticed that his eyes were the most unusual shade of greeny-grey. In fact, she stared at them for so long that she was not listening to what he was saying to her.

"Lady Novella?" he repeated, peering at the rumpled vision in front of him.

"Oh, I am sorry, Sir Edward, what was it you were saying?"

"I said that since we last met I have done nothing but think about what you said about wanting to see Salamander again, so I have come to make sure that you realised that my invitation to my stables was genuine. I think we said Wednesday? That is tomorrow, would you be kind enough to say yes? Please, Lady Novella, I feel I have to make amends to you."

The way he looked at her – so deep and meaningful – made Novella's heart skip a beat.

'I cannot possibly fraternise with a man who is a friend of my stepfather and who bought Papa's horses without a second thought – to accept would be disloyal – ' she considered.

But before she could stop herself, she heard herself saying,

"I would love to, thank you, Sir Edward."

"In that case, I shall expect you after luncheon. Good

day, Lady Novella."

He put on his hat, took Novella's hand and kissed it, all the while looking deep into her eyes.

Novella felt a shiver deep down inside as his lips touched her fingers – it was as if she had been jolted into life by a huge bolt of lightning. The feeling was something like the thrill she experienced when taking a jump with Salamander. But no, it was more than that –

Pulling her hand back as if she had been burnt, Novella was shocked to feel her heart beating quite so fast.

'Why does he make me feel like this?' she thought, as they stood there in silence.

"Let me show you to the door," offered Novella hurriedly. She was anxious to regain her composure, even though she felt inwardly in a turmoil.

'It is just that I am excited at seeing Salamander – yes, that will be it,' she said to herself as they walked towards the door.

"Until Wednesday afternoon, then?"

"Yes, until Wednesday – "

Turning sharply, she hurried back down the hallway. Her first thought was to go upstairs to wash and change.

'I need to lie down for a while, that will make me feel better,' she told herself.

But had she stopped on the doorstep and turned around, she would have seen Sir Edward craning his neck all the way down the drive in an attempt to catch one last glimpse of her –

CHAPTER SIX

The rest of the day passed in a something of a haze for Novella. Almost as soon as Sir Edward had left, she walked upstairs to wash and change and instead found herself falling asleep – completely clothed – on her bed.

'The letter to Doctor von Haydn!' she cried upon waking, suddenly remembering that she had still to finish and send it.

Running back to her father's study, she withdrew the letter from the desk drawer and completed it as soon as she could. Although she did not have time to go to the Post Office herself, she wandered out to the stables to see if Ned would take it for her.

"My Lady, how is her Ladyship?" asked Charles, as soon as he saw her approaching.

"Still very much the same. Actually, I have an errand for Ned, would you be able to spare him a while?"

"Of course, my Lady. What would you have him do for you?"

Novella handed Charles the letter.

"It is very important – it is for the specialist from London who knows much about chest complaints. I am hoping that he will be able to find out what ails Mama."

"Then Ned shall go at once, my Lady! Here you are, boy, Bluebell can go back into the field. Take Folly, she's been champing at the bit all afternoon to get out for a gallop."

"Still as lively as ever, is she?"

"To be sure, my Lady. Sir Edward missed a trick when he passed over 'er! She's still got plenty of life in 'er for an old one."

Novella smiled to herself.

"Very good, Charles. Please ask Ned to make all haste to the village, that letter is urgent. The sooner Doctor von Haydn gets here, the better."

*

Novella knew that she could not avoid having dinner with her stepfather alone for a second evening, so she steeled herself for another unpleasant experience.

Such had her dislike of him grown, that it pained her to be in the same room as him for any length of time.

She entered the dining room with her heart banging against her ribs, so she was relieved to see that Lord Buckton had yet to appear.

'I hope he is with Mama,' she thought, as she sat down.

Lily immediately brought her an empty plate.

"Lord Buckton has asked for you to wait for him before starting," she said, as she moved away from the table.

So, Novella sat with folded hands in her lap for some twenty minutes.

Her stomach was just beginning to let out low grumbles of hunger when the door of the dining room swung open and in walked Lord Buckton.

He did not impart a single word of greeting, merely inclining his head slightly before sitting down with a grunt at the table.

"Shall I serve now, my Lord?" asked Lily nervously.

It was plain to see that the servants were all terrified of the man for Lily's hand shook as she placed a helping of caviar on toast in front of him.

"Give me another portion, you stupid girl," he snapped, looking with disdain at the modest amount that had been set before him.

"Lord Buckton may have mine," said Novella, "I have no taste for caviar."

"Too good for you, is it? he answered, as he pushed one half of the toast into his mouth.

"Not at all. It is just not to my liking."

"I wonder, Lady Novella, what is to *your* liking, apart from horses? And horses, fine as they may be, will not bring offers of marriage flocking in."

"I have no wish to marry yet awhile, I have only just returned to Crownley Hall," retorted Novella, as calmly as she could.

"And the longer you hang around your mother's skirts, the more unlikely it is that you will find a suitor. I shall make some enquiries as to suitable young gentlemen the next time I visit London."

Novella was quite aware of where this conversation was leading.

"And I suppose you have some relative somewhere, who would be right for me?" she suggested sarcastically.

"Does the prospect of being part of my family displease you, madam?" he replied, glaring at her.

Novella decided that it was best if she tried to change the topic of conversation.

"How was Mama when you called in on her?"

"Much the same," came the indifferent answer.

"I do so hope that the specialist will be able to help

her."

"I beg your pardon? I had thought that I had forbidden you to send for him."

"Mama needs to see someone."

"If I say she is fine, then she is fine. A specialist would be a waste of money and we have precious little enough of that to go spending on quacks and witchdoctors!"

"Doctor von Haydn is a well-respected professional and I see that we have money enough for expensive appetisers – "

"Enough!" her stepfather shouted, spittle from his mouth landing inches away from her plate. "If you have money to throw around, then, as I have told you before, you should give it to me. There are certain pressing debts which I have to pay, so you will kindly make funds available to me."

Novella looked down at her plate – she was tired of the same conversation each time she sat down to dinner with her stepfather, but on this occasion, she did not answer him.

'*It is always about money!*' she thought to herself.

She glanced over to where Lily was standing terrified. Novella could see that the poor girl did not know whether or not to take their plates away.

"Lily, you may clear the table."

The maid hurriedly gathered up their plates – almost as if she was afraid of Lord Buckton throwing something at her – and then brought the main course of roasted pheasant with cress.

As Novella ate, she could see her stepfather growing angrier.

"I repeat, if you have money from an unknown source with which to pay this doctor, then I wish to know of it."

Still Novella declined to reply.

It was the final straw for Lord Buckton. Smashing down his forkful of pheasant with a noisy clatter, he yelled,

"You will answer me! Where does this money come from? I order you to tell me."

And then he banged his hand down on the table so hard that Novella's glass jumped into the air before crashing at her feet in a thousand pieces.

"Oh, Lummy!" cried Lily, rushing over to the broken glass.

"Go and fetch a dustpan and brush, Lily," ordered Novella, quietly.

"Sir, you have made it abundantly clear that you cannot or will not pay for Mama's care and as it is in my power to do, I shall not hesitate in meeting the expense from my own pocket. My money is mine to do with what I will."

And with that, she swept out of the dining room, her stepfather shouting at her all the way whilst poor Lily vanished in search of something to sweep up the mess.

*

After breakfast the next morning, which Novella ate from a tray in her mother's room, she sat eagerly looking out of the window in the hope that Doctor von Haydn would appear on the horizon.

She had told him in her letter not to waste time on a reply but to proceed directly to the Hall as soon as he could.

"Novella, dear, are you there?"

Turning sharply away from the window, Novella hurried to her mother's side.

The Countess looked paler than ever and her eyes were sunken. She appeared to be having great difficulty in breathing.

"What is it, Mama?"

"I would dearly like to have a drink of barley-water, is

there some on the sideboard?"

"No, I will have to go down to the kitchen to fetch some, Mama."

Novella did not waste a moment longer, she ran downstairs and into the kitchen. Lily was shocked to see her below stairs.

"My Lady?" she cried, her arms buried in the large sink as she was washing the breakfast plates.

"It is all right, Lily, I have just come for some barley-water. Where does Mrs. Armitage keep it?"

"There is a batch in the larder, my Lady. She made some first thing this morning."

It had been quite some time since Novella had last been in the larder and as she opened the door, the smell of yeast wafted up.

"Ah, here it is," she said, alighting upon a brown, earthenware jug with a muslin cover.

By the time she returned upstairs, the Countess had drifted off to sleep. Novella poured a glass of the cloudy liquid from the jug and placed it by her mother's bedside.

'Once Mrs. Armitage returns, I shall go and make my riding habit ready,' she said to herself not without a small note of satisfaction.

For today was the day she would see her beloved Salamander once more!

While she waited for Mrs. Armitage to relieve her, she returned once more to the window. It was a beautiful day and the sun was shining. The blossom was just about beginning to burst upon the cherry trees at the end of the garden.

The pretty blossom filled Novella's heart with hope for the future.

*

It was just after luncheon and Novella was about to go to the stables to pick up Bluebell for the ride over to Sir Edward's house, when Lily came rushing out with her cap askew.

"My Lady, my Lady! There is a Mr. Gross in the hall for you – he says he has come to look at the West wing."

Novella did not waste any time, she hurried inside to meet Mr. Gross.

"I am sorry I did not send word, my Lady, but I was in the neighbourhood and thought to call and make a start, if it is convenient."

"Well, I am about to go out, but let me take you to see the West wing."

Novella led him along the corridor to the ruined set of rooms that made up the West wing.

"As you can see, it is has been allowed to fall into a terrible state."

As Novella left, she reminded Mr. Gross that should her stepfather intervene, then he should say that she was bearing the cost.

However as Novella was about to leave the West wing, her stepfather came thundering in. Seeing Lord Buckton approaching, Mr. Gross shooed his men out of the side door and followed suit.

"What is all this? Who are these men?" shouted her stepfather.

"I cannot allow the Hall to fall down around my ears and as you have refused to meet the expense, I am paying for the work myself, out of my own pocket," responded Novella stoutly.

And with that, she turned to go.

But Lord Buckton was not going to allow matters to rest there – he rushed up to Novella and grabbed her by the wrist.

"You will tell me where all this money is coming from, my Lady, or you will live to regret it."

"Please! Stop! You are hurting me," cried Novella, trying to free herself.

But Lord Buckton, although elderly, was still a strong man – he clung onto her wrist, twisting the delicate flesh until it turned white.

"You *will* tell me who is giving you this money, for I cannot believe that you have some vast fund of your own."

By now tears were springing up in Novella's eyes. Try as she might, she could not free herself from his vice-like grip.

"Let me go, I beg of you!" she pleaded.

"Then, tell me."

Thankfully, just at that moment, Mrs. Armitage appeared. She took one look at Novella attempting to twist herself free from Lord Buckton and a look of horror crossed her face.

"My Lord, your carriage is waiting for you. You will miss your appointment."

Lord Buckton paused for a moment and then freed his grip on Novella's wrist.

"We will speak of this again later," he snarled, spittle issuing forth from his lips.

Almost in a swoon, Novella staggered towards the hallway. Viewing her harassed expression in the mirror, she straightened her hat and took several deep breaths.

She stood there for some moments, before she gathered herself together and proceeded towards Charles, Ned and Bluebell.

"She's a bit skittish, my Lady," Ned said, holding Bluebell steady as Charles helped her up into the saddle.

"Be careful, my Lady," urged Charles, as Novella dug her heels into Bluebell's side – and she had the distinct feeling he was not only referring to the ride ahead of her.

*

Once Novella was out of the grounds of Crownley Hall, she felt an immense load lifting from her shoulders. Racing across the fields was good for her and she became more of her old self.

'Out here, I feel free,' she thought, as the gates of Sir Edward's house came into view.

It was not as grand as Crownley Hall, but still possessed a graceful air. The Moretons were an old family who lived off their ancestors' fortune made in the British Empire. Sir Edward's grandfather had worked for the East India Company.

Novella had always longed to see Tithehurst and, as Bluebell trotted through the gates, she could see Sir Edward standing at the front of the house as if waiting for someone.

"Lady Novella!" he shouted in greeting, a brilliant smile on his face. "Proceed to the stables, you will find them behind the house. Salamander is waiting for you!"

A groom came rushing up to her as she drew up to the stables and caught Bluebell by the bridle.

"Where is Salamander?" she asked breathlessly, as she climbed down.

"In the stall at the far end, my Lady," said the groom, leading Bluebell away for a tasty bundle of hay and a bucket of water.

"Salamander! *Salamander!*" cried Novella, anxiously scanning the stables for her horse.

A loud whinny alerted her to the presence of her favourite steed. He poked his head out of the stable door and whinnied once more.

"*Salamander!*"

Novella did not wait, she ran up to the horse and threw her arms around his strong neck. He was clearly as delighted to see her as she was him.

"You beautiful, wonderful darling!" she called, crying with joy, "I have missed you so much"

"In that case, you must come and see him as often as you can. As you can see, he is a very healthy chap," came a voice from behind her.

Novella turned to see Sir Edward, looking incredibly handsome in his riding gear, standing there.

"Why, thank you very much," replied Novella, quite taken aback.

'He is not at all like my stepfather,' she thought, as Sir Edward produced a carrot from his pocket and fed it to Salamander. 'He is so kind and thoughtful.'

As if he read her mind, Sir Edward chuckled before saying,

"You might wonder how I know Lord Buckton when there are so many years between us. I was at school with his nephew, John. We used to spend the summers at the Buckton's old estate – "

"The estate which he sold when he married Mama," added Novella. "Although there is precious little evidence of the money he must have gained from that deal – "

Sir Edward gave a wry smile.

"I expect you are eager to take Salamander out. Come, my horse is ready and it will not take long for him to be saddled up."

Novella did not need any further encouragement. She followed Sir Edward to the front of the stables where she would mount her horse.

"My saddle!" she cried, upon seeing Salamander

sporting the very same one that Sir Edward had taken away only a few days previously.

"I did try to explain, Lady Novella, that I was only taking it so that you might ride him, but I think you feared the worst and so I didn't get a chance to tell you."

'I am a silly fool,' she thought, as she climbed up onto the box that had been brought out to help her mount.

Presently, the groom brought round a fine, coal-black stallion for Sir Edward.

"Shall we head for the river?" he asked, settling down in the saddle.

One touch of Novella's whip and Salamander was off!

As they galloped across the fields, Salamander was yards ahead of Sir Edward's mount.

"Come on, boy," urged Novella, as she saw the silvery line of the river in the distance.

Half an hour later, she arrived at the river with Sir Edward still trailing behind her. Salamander was dripping with sweat as Novella jumped down and then led him towards the cool water.

"There you are, my boy, drink all you can."

"I am afraid I cannot keep up with you!" puffed Sir Edward, dismounting, "you are a very fine horsewoman, Lady Novella."

"Please, just call me Novella" she told him smiling, "there is no need to be so formal up here."

Leaving Salamander drinking in the river, Novella walked along the grassy banks.

"I have so many happy memories of this place."

"I also," admitted Sir Edward, coming alongside her.

"Papa used to bring me here every summer whenever he had the time. We would swim and have a picnic. Up here, he was not the Earl but a father enjoying time with his daughter."

"You must miss him very much," ventured Sir Edward.

"Yes, I do. And now I fear for Mama – she is not at all well."

"You have called the doctor, of course?"

"He came to the Hall but could not help Mama. So I have sent for a specialist from London – a Doctor von Haydn. I am waiting for him to attend Mama – "

"Do you think it is serious?"

"I know it is as otherwise Doctor Jones would have been able to treat her. I confess I fear the worst."

Sir Edward gazed at her intently, his greeny-grey eyes full of concern.

"How are you managing?"

"You mean now that my stepfather has dismissed most of the servants?"

"I – "

"There is no need to apologise, Sir Edward, I realise that the situation at the Hall is common knowledge around the village and beyond. I discovered that upon visiting some of the local tradesmen."

"Lord Buckton is a man who is fond of the material things in life."

"He cares nothing for Mama! That much I do know."

By now, Novella was close to tears. Sir Edward advanced slowly towards her, almost as if he was about to take her hand and then he stopped short.

Novella continued to talk, so grateful at having a sympathetic ear.

"It is obvious that my stepfather dislikes me intensely, but that does not prevent him from attempting to obtain my money. Papa left enough for Mama and me to live in comfort, but we find ourselves far from that blissful state."

Sir Edward paused and then spoke,

"It is always difficult when a parent remarries. I have friends who have found themselves in most awkward situations after such an event. Fortunately, after my mother died, my father had no wish to spend his life with any other and he remained a grieving widower until he died. It was a huge shock when he passed away and I was not ready for the responsibility of running a house and these modest grounds. I cannot imagine how you must feel with the burden of Crownley Hall upon your shoulders."

Novella looked at Sir Edward and a sudden tenderness sprang into her heart.

"You seem to understand how I feel about Crownley Hall – " she murmured.

"It is obvious to anyone who meets you that you love the Hall as much as you do your Mama and Salamander!"

Sir Edward laughed as he patted Salamander on the flank, as he was grazing contentedly on the river bank.

It had been a long time since Novella had felt so happy – and she found herself completely at ease in Sir Edward's company.

Novella was well aware that she had little experience of dealing socially with the opposite sex outside of friendship. There had been a few would-be suitors who called at her lodgings at the school, but her maid had always sent them away, saying she was not at home.

Novella had never been in love and she could not imagine what it might feel like.

But standing on the riverbank, watching Sir Edward playing with Salamander, she felt a mysterious yearning in her heart that she could not explain.

'I must not indulge myself in silly notions,' she thought, shaking herself. 'I must not allow myself to be distracted from Mama and Crownley Hall.'

Nevertheless, she could not deny that she felt a strange, haunting longing and a secret thrill at being in Sir Edward's company.

"We should be moving on," she suggested, drawing Salamander close to her, "will you please help me up?"

After a long and exhausting ride, the sun began to sink in the sky and Sir Edward suggested that they should return to Tithehurst.

"It is growing late," he told her, "and you have to ride home afterwards."

They rode back in silence with Novella in turmoil. She could not understand why she felt so – was it just because she had not ridden Salamander for so long or was it something to do with Sir Edward?

"Would you care to stay for tea?" asked Sir Edward, as they rode through the gates of Tithehurst.

"I should return to the Hall," replied Novella, "in case Doctor von Haydn has arrived."

"In that case, you must promise me that you will come again. You are free to ride Salamander whenever you please."

It was with a heavy heart and a few tears that Novella said goodbye to Salamander.

"I will come again soon, I promise you," she breathed, stroking his silky mane.

She said a hasty farewell to Sir Edward and then climbed back onto Bluebell.

"Come on, girl," she entreated, as the mare trotted towards Crownley Hall.

'After Salamander, I feel as if I am mounted on a

garden slug,' sighed Novella, trying her best to coax Bluebell to go faster.

*

Arriving back at Crownley Hall, Novella felt herself to be utterly spent. Until she climbed down from Bluebell, she had not realised how unfit she had become.

'I will return to Salamander,' she resolved, 'I cannot leave it so long again.'

Walking back towards the house, Novella noticed that Mr. Gross's cart was no longer standing outside.

'How strange,' she thought. 'Surely he was not put off by my stepfather?'

The answer soon became apparent, as no sooner had she stepped inside, than Lord Buckton had appeared in the doorway of the drawing room holding a fine new cane that Novella had not seen before.

"What was the meaning of that builder prowling around the Tower this afternoon?" he growled before she had a chance to greet him.

Drawing herself up to her full height, Novella replied,

"I have paid Mr. Gross in advance to take the broken gargoyles away so that he could carve some new ones."

"Well, you can go straight there tomorrow and take them back! Tell him that we have no need of his over-priced services."

"Sir, you have no right!" she fumed, "as I am paying the bills, I fail to see what concern it is of yours what I do to the house."

"How dare you!" he raged, coming towards her in a most threatening manner. "How dare you commission these people without my say-so. I am the man of Crownley Hall, not you. Kindly remember that in future."

"It is my money and I will do with it what I will and if

I wish to spend it on the house rather than fine gowns, then that is my concern. I was here long before you, Lord Buckton, and I do not see you hurrying to repair the Hall when it is falling down around your ears."

"You will do as I say." bawled Lord Buckton, throwing his silver-topped cane down the hallway at her. "I have warned you before about this ridiculous attempt to keep from me what is mine by rights. If you have money to throw around, then, as your guardian, I am entitled to take it from you."

Novella found herself frozen to the spot. She was exhausted from her ride and was unable to move. Lord Buckton began to stride towards her, but suddenly the loud clattering of the doorbell interrupted them.

"Is Lady Novella Crownley at home?"

A wave of relief swept over Novella as she heard the heavily accented voice. It could be no one but Doctor von Haydn.

"Please, come in, doctor! I am so glad to see you!" cried Novella, rushing forward to greet him.

She shook his hand warmly and immediately liked the look of the small, rounded gentleman in the tall hat and checked overcoat. He carried a black bag and leaned forward, as if in a hurry, when he walked.

As Novella passed Lord Buckton, he grabbed her.

"I will deal with you later, you can be certain of *that*," he growled in a low menacing voice.

"Please come with me, doctor," invited Novella, trying not to show how shaken she was. "Mama is upstairs."

She could feel Lord Buckton's eyes boring into her back as she accompanied the doctor to her mother's room.

'I am in serious trouble,' she thought, as she closed the door behind her, '*very serious trouble indeed.*'

CHAPTER SEVEN

Novella waited patiently outside her mother's room while Doctor von Haydn was inside examining her.

With her stepfather's words ringing in her ears, she eerily recalled how her old maid Sally had feared that both her and her mother's lives were in danger.

What was it she said?

'Lord Buckton will stop at nothing to get his hands on the Hall.'

'Surely, he would not stoop to murder?' she thought again, as she paced up and down the corridor. 'Perhaps Mama's illness has been brought upon her by some dastardly means!'

And so, Novella's mind ran riot until the moment that Doctor von Haydn opened the door and beckoned her forth.

"My Lady, I am afraid it is not good news. Your mother has a tumour – quite a rare kind, too. It is on her lungs and I am afraid that it is too far gone for me to be able to help. All she needs now is round-the-clock nursing and a good diet – and your prayers, of course."

Novella went white with shock.

"Will – will Mama die?"

"The prognosis is not good. But we can always hope for a miracle. Whatever she asks for, however strange, do not hesitate to let her have it."

"Oh, Mama. No! *No!*" cried Novella, "I only lost my Papa two years ago and now this. It is too much!"

She broke into sobs and the poor doctor did not know what he should do with her. He stood there, quite stiff, about a yard away from her.

"Shall I send for the maid?" he asked, as he watched the young girl crying.

"No, no, I shall be all right presently," whimpered Novella, pulling herself together. "Your news does not come as a complete surprise. It is just so hard to hear you say the words."

"I understand, my Lady. Now, if there is anything else I can do for you, you must send for me urgently. Should her Ladyship become worse, I will come at once."

"Thank you so very much, doctor," replied Novella, feeling a little stupid for having such wild imaginings about her stepfather.

Novella saw him to the door and as she did so noticed that Charles was outside.

"Did Lord Buckton say when he might be back?"

"Yes, my Lady – tomorrow morning, I believe."

Walking back inside, Novella was angry.

'Most likely he has gone to visit his lady-friend,' she fumed, returning to her mother's bedroom. 'The man has not one shred of decency in his entire body!'

Mrs. Armitage was back at the Countess's side, so Novella simply kissed her sleeping mother and retired for the night.

'I shall engage a nurse and buy her whatever she needs,' she resolved, as she brushed out her long hair. 'Mama shall not want for anything while I have it in my power to grant it.'

The next day passed slowly. Novella found herself unable to concentrate on anything for very long and it was not just because her mother was becoming progressively worse.

As the long afternoon wore on, she found herself thinking more and more about Sir Edward Moreton.

'He certainly cut a fine figure on a horse,' she mused, as she remembered him astride his handsome, black stallion.

Novella admired good horsemen – her father had been almost without equal in the County and she had been put upon a horse before she could barely walk.

'I almost do not mind a man such as Sir Edward buying our horses now I have seen how much he cares for them,' she thought, as she sat idly in the drawing room.

'My stepfather may have ill-treated them and I could not have borne that.'

She allowed the book she was attempting to read fall into her lap and began to daydream. She relived each second she had spent on Salamander and the conversation she had so enjoyed with Sir Edward.

'He seemed to really understand my predicament,' she said to herself, 'I have never felt so comfortable with anyone outside of my own family.'

And then she realised what she had been dreaming and picked her book up once more.

It was a torrid tale by Mrs. Henry Wood about a village not unlike Crownley and an estate not unlike that of the Hall.

As she read the story of how one Lady Isabel only discovered how much she loved her husband once terrible calamity had befallen her, Novella put it back down again, puzzling furiously to herself.

'Is that how love can be? That one can be unaware of

how much a person means to you until they are out of one's reach? Oh, how I wish Mama was well and she could explain why I feel so upset today.'

It did indeed occur to her that perhaps she might be entertaining a secret desire for Sir Edward.

'How would I feel if he suddenly announced that he was to be married? Would I, too, as Lady Isabel does in the story, only realise when it was too late, that I cared for him?'

She sighed heavily and then became quite cross with herself.

'But this is only a stupid story and I cannot imagine that love is like that. How silly. I am sure I should know when I was in love with someone and when I was not.'

She was grateful that her stepfather had yet to return – it had made luncheon, although frugal, much more pleasant. Novella hoped fervently that he would still be out for dinner, although it made her blood boil that he was so faithless to her mother at a time when she most needed him.

In fact, she had avoided going into her mother's room that day unless she knew she was asleep – for each time, the Countess asked for her husband and Novella was forced to lie and say he was in Stockington.

There had been a marked decline in the Countess's health since the doctor's visit, and more than once that day, Novella wondered if she should call Doctor von Haydn back – or send for Doctor Jones.

She had written to an agency in London for a nurse to look after her mother and she hoped that she would not have to wait long.

The day slid by until just after seven and Novella was about to go and change for dinner when a hand-delivered message arrived at the Hall for her. Lily brought it to her in the drawing room.

"What is this?" she asked, as the girl handed her the

creamy paper.

"A messenger from Tithehurst brought it, my Lady. He has not waited for a reply but has left."

'How strange,' murmured Novella, pulling the seal off the paper and reading it.

"*My dear Lady Novella,*

I shall not forget our wonderful ride across the country together for a very long time. I enjoyed your company immensely and hope to do so again in the near future. In the meantime, as soon as you have read this note, I would entreat you to visit the stables, for there you will find a small token of my esteem.

The invitation to visit Tithehurst whenever you wish remains there for you. I fervently hope that I shall be honoured with your company in the near future.

Yours sincerely,

Edward Moreton."

Novella pondered the contents of the letter for a few moments until her curiosity got the better of her.

Even though it was getting dark outside, she took a lantern, lit it and then proceeded to the stables.

'Perhaps he has sent back my saddle,' she speculated, 'or even bought me a new one.'

As soon as she rounded the corner, she could see Charles standing there – a huge grin spread across his face like someone had just given him a sack of gold.

"My Lady! *Come with me!*"

"What is it, Charles?"

"You wait and see, my Lady."

They went inside the stables and then, moving ahead of her, he beckoned her to follow him into the end stall.

'How very curious,' thought Novella.

But as she inched nearer, she heard a very familiar snort. Scarcely able to believe her own ears, she rushed the last few yards and there, in his old stall, was Salamander!

"Oh, I cannot believe it!" she cried, throwing her arms around the horse's neck.

"Look there, my Lady. There is a note on his bridle. I cannot read so I don't know what it says. Perhaps it will tell us why dear old Salamander has come home?"

Novella tore the label off Salamander's bridle.

It said.

"My lady, after seeing how magnificently you rode Salamander the other afternoon, I have come to the conclusion that he would be ruined if anyone else mounted him. So I have decided to send him back home to his rightful owner. Consider it a gift to a very talented, very beautiful horsewoman who has no equal in this or any other County."

"How very generous!" exclaimed Novella, taking off Salamander's bridle so that he could feel free. 'And Sir Edward thinks I am beautiful.'

She was aware that those words had caused a strange feeling to well up inside her. It was not at all unpleasant –

But her reverie was broken by the sound of clattering hooves and the grinding of wheels. It was Lord Buckton with a face like thunder.

"Why is that brute stabled here?" he shouted, "I thought I had sold him, so kindly explain why he is eating my hay and taking advantage of my shelter?"

Her stepfather jumped down from the carriage and as he did so, Novella swore she could smell the scent of Parma violets upon him.

"Sir Edward has kindly sent him over on extended loan so that I might once again enjoy riding him," she retorted, feeling that if she had a shovel nearby, she would hit him with it should he try to send Salamander back.

"What stuff and nonsense is this? What ails the man?"

"If you are worrying about Salamander's upkeep, I will make sure that nothing he touches is paid for by you, so you should not concern yourself unduly."

Lord Buckton smiled – a terrible smile of triumph.

"We shall see about what you do or don't have, my Lady. For this very day I have been to see my own solicitor – not that pair of dolts your family employs – and it appears that I have a very good claim on whatever money is in your bank account. What is yours is mine as I am your mother's husband, and once she goes, then it will all belong to me!"

"You – you heartless beast!" shouted Novella, fury in her eyes. "Do you care nothing about Mama's health? We are going to lose her and all you are concerned with is money!"

With that, she stormed off back towards the house, leaving her stepfather to laugh loudly at her retreat.

'Who does he think he is?' she raged, as she slammed shut her bedroom door. 'Mr. Longridge will not allow him access to my account, even if he threatens him with a shotgun. The man is quite clearly out of his mind."

She rang for Lily and asked her to bring her dinner on a tray and then looked in on her mother.

The Countess was awake but feeling weak.

"The nurse will be here very soon," said Novella, soothingly, as she plumped up the pillows. "And then you shall not have to spend a moment on your own."

It was not long before she was fast asleep. Novella watched her for a while and then she heard Lily's footsteps outside. Remembering that she had asked for her dinner to be taken to her room, she tiptoed out so as not to disturb her mother.

'I shall have an early night and then ride Salamander in the morning,' she muttered as she finished her dinner, 'perhaps I shall visit Tithehurst and thank Sir Edward personally. Yes, I shall do that tomorrow – '

*

Novella was so exhausted that she slept extremely well. Awaking the next morning, she felt she would be able to face whatever the day threw at her.

She got up, washed and dressed and then, turning the doorknob, she found that it was shut fast.

'How peculiar, perhaps it has become stuck in the night,' she thought.

But try as she might, she could not open the door.

Eventually the truth dawned on her as she looked at the lock and saw that the key was no longer there.

'My stepfather must have had me locked in. Fool that I am, I quite forgot to take the key yesterday before I went out. No doubt, on his instructions, Mrs. Armitage took it and gave it to him, and so as soon as I was asleep, he came and locked it.'

Novella was in tears of frustration as she wondered what she should do. There were a few, dry crusts still on her plate from last night and some water in the carafe beside her bed, so she would not go totally hungry or thirsty.

Even so, Novella was incensed that her stepfather had taken this measure.

'*How dare he!*' she thought, as she tried to think of a way to get out.

Walking over to the window, she looked down at the long drop below.

'No, I should certainly kill myself if I attempted to climb out of the window,' she reasoned.

"What shall I do? *What shall I do?*" she cried, pacing

back and forth.

'What does he seek to achieve by confining me to my room? I have already sent for the nurse to look after Mama and Doctor von Haydn has been and pronounced his verdict – I can only assume he hopes to control me by doing this.'

And that thought, so repellent to Novella, made her cry hot tears of frustration.

"I will not allow him to control me, *I will not*," she screamed, as she hit the bedding with her fist.

'I expect he will now be attempting to gain access to my bank account,' she thought grimly, wiping away her tears.

'I have heard no one at the door this morning, so the nurse cannot have arrived yet. For that, I must be grateful at least for I am certain that he would send her away.'

The realisation that she could not go to see her mother played heavily on Novella's mind and very soon she began to cry.

'Supposing Mama has died in the night? Would Mrs. Armitage come to fetch me?' she thought, miserably.

Eventually, worn out with emotion, she lay on the bed and began to doze.

She did not know how long she slept, but was awoken some time later by the sound of voices in the hallway outside and the turning of the key in the lock.

'It will be Mrs. Armitage, come to give me news of Mama,' felt Novella, sitting up sleepily.

So she was most dismayed to find her stepfather standing over her.

"Now, let us see if a little confinement has subdued you," he growled, in a low menacing voice. "I have here a paper from my solicitor and if you will kindly sign it, then I will be able to gain access to your bank account. He has informed me that unless you do so, I cannot make any withdrawals."

He proffered the paper.

"Never. *Never*. That money is for Mama and me and the house – it is not for you to fritter away on new carriages and fancy women!"

Lord Buckton stared at her long and hard.

"Then I see that you shall have to stay put for a while longer. I will leave the paper here for you and by the time I return I expect you to have signed it. Mrs. Armitage will bring you a luncheon tray. Now, I shall need a little down payment for something I intend to purchase."

Novella sat helpless while her stepfather walked purposefully over to her dressing table and began to rifle in her jewellery box.

"Ah, this will do," he declared, picking up a diamond pendant.

"But that is the necklace Uncle Richard bought me for my sixteenth birthday."

"And it is far too fine for a girl like you to wear. Yes, I will take it and let that be a lesson to you. The sooner you realise that everything in Crownley Hall is mine for the taking, the better."

With that, he strode off and let himself out, locking the door firmly behind him.

'The brute!' cried Novella, 'it is the only present I have from Mama's brother who is now dead.'

But she realised that she was powerless to stop him. Until she found a way out of her room, she could not go for help. It did cross her mind to go to Tithehurst but she dismissed it instantly.

'I still do not know if I can trust Sir Edward,' she murmured, 'no, Mr. Longridge is my only hope. The only problem is how to get out of my room.'

Feeling defeated, she sank back down on the bed and waited.

But just then, shouts outside made her run back to the window.

There, walking along the rear garden path were Charles and Folly!

Folly was in one of her skittish moods and kept rearing up, much to Charles's annoyance.

Novella thought quickly and then, without hesitating, threw open the window.

Although she knew it was unladylike to shout, she yelled as loud as her lungs would permit.

"Charles! Charles!"

She could see the groom's head turning, trying to locate where the sound was coming from. He looked puzzled.

'Oh, goodness,' said Novella to herself, 'he probably does not know that I am up here. He would not expect me to behave in such an uncouth way.'

So she shouted again.

"Charles! Charles! Look up. I am on the third floor."

"My Lady!" he cried, "what on earth are you doing of?"

"I am locked in, Charles. I cannot get out of my room."

"Is this *his* doing?" he asked, with a frown.

"I fear so."

"What can I do to get you out? I can't get up a ladder, my Lady, my legs are too bad for that and young Ned is out with Bluebell."

Novella thought for a second – Mr. Longridge could help.

"Charles, could you ride immediately to Stockington and go and see Mr. Hubert Longridge at the bank? Tell him what has happened and ask him to come here with all haste."

Charles did not hesitate – he grabbed Folly by the bridle and began to drag her towards the stables.

"Don't worry, my Lady. I'll saddle up this little madam and go straight away. Come on, Folly, we've got important business!"

Novella sank back down on the bed and prepared herself for a long wait. Even if Charles left at once, it would still be some hours before he returned.

'I do hope that Mr. Longridge will arrive before my stepfather returns home,' she said to herself. 'Without his intervention, I fear that Lord Buckton will somehow find a way to gain access to the money that Papa left.

'Oh, dear God! *Hear me.* If ever anyone needed your help right now – here I am. How I pray that you are listening!'

And with that prayer, she reconciled herself to a long wait.

CHAPTER EIGHT

As promised, Mrs. Armitage brought Novella her luncheon on a tray but did not even put her head in the door. She simply unlocked it and quickly pushed the tray through the crack.

Novella had considered attempting to force the door back, but she felt too tired and weak.

"How is Mama?" she shouted as she heard the lock snapping fast once more.

But no reply came from Mrs. Armitage.

The sun had begun its long descent in the sky by the time that Novella once again heard the sound of horse's hooves outside.

Then came the voice that immediately made her feel better –

"My Lady! My Lady! We are back and I've brought Mr. Longridge with me."

Standing down in the garden, looking pleased with himself, was Charles.

"Where is he?" Novella cried, unable to see neither hide nor hair of Mr. Longridge.

"He be in his carriage at the front."

"Charles, will you ask him to go at once to Mrs. Armitage and demand that she lets me out of my room?"

"Right away, my Lady."

It seemed to take forever before she heard the sound of her bedroom door being unlocked. The door flew open and in walked Mr. Longridge, wearing an anxious look on his face.

"Lady Novella! Are you harmed?"

Novella ran up to him and took his hand, squeezing it warmly.

"I am quite well, thank you. A little upset, but apart from that, I am fine."

"What was that devil thinking of? Locking you in your own room?"

"He is attempting to gain access to my bank account and thinks that if he confines me, I will sign *this*."

Novella handed him the sheet of paper that her stepfather had left earlier.

"Well," said Mr. Longridge, after reading it, "I am no solicitor but I cannot see that this will help him in his quest. I think you will find that your father's will is watertight and no amount of so-called clever lawyers will be able to make it otherwise."

"That is such a relief," murmured Novella, "now, come please to Papa's library – it is not safe to speak freely here."

Novella noticed that Mrs. Armitage had pocketed the key to her room again and it made her feel uneasy.

Opening the door to her father's library, Novella ushered in Mr. Longridge. He looked round appreciatively.

"Ah, yes, very much your father's taste. But where is the painting of the hunt at Thaxby?"

"I fear it has been sold, like many other valuable commodities in this house."

"The man is a scoundrel!" exclaimed Mr. Longridge,

sitting down in the comfortable leather chair that Novella offered him. "And I repeat, you really must have no fears that he will be able lay his hands on your father's secret fund – it is beyond his reach."

"I am very glad of that. But there is one thing that puzzles me."

"Pray tell, what is that?"

"I am mystified as to how you persuaded Mrs. Armitage to let me out of my room. She is so scared of my stepfather that she does whatever he commands. The only time she defies him – and it is not really true defiance – is when she sits with my Mama for hours at a time, nursing her. Otherwise, she is completely in Lord Buckton's thrall. It is as if he had some power over her – "

"The power to turn her over to an Officer of the law, I'll be bound."

Novella looked at him in astonishment.

"What do you mean?"

"I have been doing a little detective work since you came to my office and I have discovered that our Mrs. Armitage has been in trouble with the law. Lord Buckton's father had her arrested over the matter of some disappearing silver. Of course, then the old Lord died and the case never went to court. So, as you can see, all I had to do was threaten to call the Police to the Hall and she capitulated."

"How very clever of you!" cried Novella, clapping her hands in delight. "I had wondered what bound her to Lord Buckton with such fierce loyalty."

"But my Lady, it is not safe for you to stay here. I would suggest that you flee for the night, if that is possible. Do you have somewhere you could go?"

"But I cannot leave Mama," she protested, "she lies seriously ill – perhaps dying."

"Lady Novella, I cannot guarantee your safety if you stay here when Lord Buckton returns. A man who would lock you up like an animal would not hesitate to go further if he comes home and finds that, not only have you been freed, but you have also refused to sign that document."

Novella thought upon his words – he was right, of course. But where could she go? She did not have a single friend in the neighbourhood apart from Sir Edward. Could she possibly turn to him in her moment of need?

"Well, Sir Edward Moreton had said that I could visit at any time to see Salamander – " she said aloud.

"He is a decent man and surely if he knew you were in danger, he would not turn you away? If you are concerned that it would not be proper – a single young lady staying with a single young gentleman – then I would imagine that his housekeeper would act as chaperone."

"No, it is not that. I am certain that Sir Edward would be the very model of gentlemanly conduct and would do nothing to put my reputation in danger – " sighed Novella, "it is the fact that he is an old friend of my stepfather's family – it would not bode well for him should he be seen to be involved with our family quarrels."

"I would not give it a second thought. Sir Edward is as discreet as he is noble."

"Allow me to see that Mama is comfortable and then I will pack a bag," she agreed at last. "Perhaps you would be good enough to drop me at Sir Edward's house after we have been to see Mr. Humbert?"

"Of course, I shall wait in the hallway for you."

Novella returned upstairs and straight away looked in on her mother. The Countess was asleep and seemed to be very peaceful.

Kissing her on the head, she bade her farewell for the time being,

"I shall see you tomorrow, Mama."

Running back to her bedroom, she quickly packed a small overnight bag and picked up her cloak. It was a warm evening, but she did not wish to catch a chill the next morning when the dew was heavy and profuse.

Mr. Longridge was waiting for her at the foot of the stairs. As she reached him, the clock chimed three.

"Come along, we must make haste," he urged, leading her to his carriage. "You will need to come to the bank with me before we take you to Sir Edward's so that you may withdraw some money. I have a feeling that you will need it."

*

It was not long before Novella found herself in the office of Rumbold and Humbert. Mr. Rumbold Junior gave them some tea and eventually they were shown into Mr. Humbert Senior's office.

"Lady Novella, to what do we owe this pleasure? Twice in one week, eh?"

Novella looked at Mr. Humbert and then back at Mr. Longridge.

"Proceed, my dear," he said, "you must tell Mr. Humbert what your stepfather has been doing."

"Mr. Humbert, I am most concerned. Lord Buckton, my stepfather, is attempting to gain access to my father's trust fund."

Mr. Humbert looked over his glasses at her and sighed,

"Then he shall be in for a long wait, Lady Novella. As I believe my colleague told you the other day, your father took most precise steps to ensure that you and your mother would be well taken care of. You do understand that should your mother die, then everything will come to you?"

"Yes, I had imagined that would be the case."

"Then let Lord Buckton do his worst – he will only find himself making one of my fellow solicitors a richer man."

"That may well be, but he has been taking extreme measures, Mr. Humbert. Only today he locked Lady Novella in her room in an attempt to force her to sign her rights away," put in an outraged Mr. Longridge.

Mr. Humbert shook his head.

"That kind of behaviour will not bring Lord Buckton what he desires. It would seem that he is trying to frighten the lady into giving up her claim. Stand firm, Lady Novella, the law is on your side."

*

As they left Mr. Humbert's office, Novella felt considerably better.

"I told you that matters were cast in your favour," remarked Mr. Longridge, as they climbed into his carriage. "Now, we should proceed with all haste to the bank. I have been away from my office for a very long time and we both have business to complete."

It did not take any time at all to arrive at the bank.

The moment he stepped inside, a harassed-looking clerk apprehended him before he had even reached as far as his office door.

"Mr. Longridge! There you are."

"What is the matter, Jones?"

"Well, sir, there has been an incident."

"What kind of incident?"

The young clerk looked nervously at Novella and lowered his voice.

"It is a somewhat delicate matter, sir."

"You may speak freely in front of Lady Novella.

Although I think I can guess what you are about to tell me. Was it Lord Buckton?"

The clerk shook his head vigorously.

"Begging your pardon, my Lady, but he was extremely violent in his manner towards the cashier. Demanded to have access to your account by virtue of him being your stepfather. Of course, we told him that unless he had a signed deposition from yourself, it would not be possible. But he flew into such a rage, smashed his cane on the counter top and clean broke it in half. Sent an inkwell flying too, he did. Mary-Anne, the secretary, was in tears so we had to send her home."

"Did you call the Police?" asked Mr. Longridge.

"No, sir, but we did threaten to do so. That seemed to calm him down a little and he left. But what a scene! Said he'd get a court order and then we'd all be in for the sack for obstructing him."

"No one will be dismissed, Jones, you can assure all your colleagues," sighed Mr. Longridge.

He then led Novella into his office in order that she could withdraw some money in peace.

"Can he really obtain a court order to gain access to my account?" asked Novella nervously, as he counted out fifty pounds in five pound notes.

"No, of course he cannot. Not unless you are certified insane or dead."

"I do believe that he would not stop at either to get what he wants!"

"And I would be here as a witness that you are both alive and in sound mind," replied Mr. Longridge. "Now, come along – we should be making our way to Sir Edward's house. I do not fancy that it will be long before Lord Buckton discovers that you are not at home and will be in hot pursuit."

Novella tucked away the money into her purse – she intended it to be payment for the nurse as soon as she arrived.

'I do hope that will not be whilst I am away from home,' she thought, as she followed Mr. Longridge back out into the street. 'It would be terrible if Lord Buckton intercepted her and turned her away. Mama needs her now more than ever. Oh, I wish I did not have to leave her.'

But she knew that if she were to regain her emotional strength to fight Lord Buckton, then she would need this short time away from Crownley Hall.

*

And so Novella and the ever-faithful Mr. Longridge journeyed over to Tithehurst. It was a warm evening and Novella had no need of the cloak she had brought with her.

The gates of the house rose up in front of them. Novella felt a curious thrill of excitement as the carriage pulled up the drive.

"I will enter the house first and ask Sir Edward if he would be good enough to extend his hospitality to you tonight," suggested Mr. Longridge, climbing down. "That way, if it is inconvenient, he will not feel awkward."

Novella sat and patiently waited.

Long moments ticked by before anything happened and then Novella caught sight of Sir Edward running towards the carriage.

"Novella. Are you all right?" he questioned, opening up the carriage door for her.

"I am fine. I assume that Mr. Longridge has told you everything?"

"Yes, he has. What a to-do. You will, of course, be staying with me tonight. I would not have it any other way."

"Thank you so much. It is such a relief to hear you say

that," she replied, leaning on his arm as she alighted from the carriage.

"My housekeeper is making the guest room ready for you. I am so glad that you came to me – you could not have stayed in that house tonight of all nights."

"I confess that I have had enough of my stepfather's ire to last me a very long time," added Novella, "my only concern is for Mama. The nurse is due to arrive at any moment and I fear that should I not be there to receive her she will be sent away."

"From what Hubert told me about your housekeeper's grumblings, I would think it likely that Mrs. Armitage would drag her back by her hair before she'd see her leave!"

Novella laughed for the first time in a long while.

"You are right. Mrs. Armitage has been nagging me constantly to find a nurse. She says that she was not hired to tend the sick."

"I think we are all agreed that your mother needs the best possible care now and I do not think even Mrs. Armitage would deny her that."

"She is a strange kettle of fish," said Novella, as they entered the elegant drawing room, "I cannot decide if she is friend or foe. She appears devoted to Mama, yet she helped Lord Buckton to imprison me in my own room. Make of that what you will – "

Sir Edward handed Novella a glass of sherry. Although she almost never drank when there was not food involved, Novella took it gratefully. She felt so at home in Sir Edward's presence that she could have easily curled up and slept right there on the sofa.

'He is a very handsome man indeed,' thought Novella, as he continued to talk about the awkward situation in which she now found herself. 'I wonder why he does not have a thousand ladies after him? Yet there has been no gossip whatsoever.'

Each time she looked at him, Novella felt her heart stirring. She was lonely and him being there for her in her hour of need only served to predispose her even more favourably towards him.

He made sure that she was comfortable and asked her what she would like for dinner.

"Oh, you must not go to any trouble on my account, I will eat whatever your cook or housekeeper is preparing for you."

"Nonsense," he protested, "I have a guest – and very dear friend dining with me tonight and so it shall be a special occasion."

"But I have not brought another gown with me," Novella pointed out, looking down in dismay at the plain, blue-silk dress with only a few pearl buttons for decoration. "This is not fine enough to grace your dining room."

"On the contrary," parried Sir Edward, smiling, "you are perfectly charmingly attired. *You look beautiful as you are.*"

Novella glanced down and blushed deeply.

But secretly, she was thrilled. Sir Edward did not take his eyes off her for a second and each look between them became more and more lingering as the evening wore on.

Novella was so unaware of the time that she did not even feel hungry until the butler came in to announce that dinner was served.

"A little late, I am afraid," said Sir Edward, offering Novella his arm.

"Goodness. It is nine o'clock already," remarked Novella, as the ornate, golden clock on the mantelpiece began to chime.

"You must be famished."

"I do believe that I am, now that you have mentioned it," she said, looking forward to spending more time alone with the dashing Sir Edward.

*

After the variable bill of fare that Novella had encountered at Crownley Hall since her return, Sir Edward's table presented a marked difference.

Each course seemed more delicious than the last and she ate heartily.

"I see that the food pleases you," commented Sir Edward, as she spooned the last morsel of a second helping of *crème bavaroise* into her mouth.

"Quite delightful," she answered, "I should like to thank your cook for providing such a wonderful meal at such short notice."

"He is a French chef, actually. His name is Jean-Charles and I found him in Paris. He was working for a cousin of mine who was about to marry into a well-to-do French family who already employed a large battery of chefs and sous-chefs. The French do take their food seriously."

"And quite right, too. But you are very lucky. There are not many households in the County who could boast a French chef."

"Ah, Lady Novella, I would not dream of boasting. It would mean that I would then be forced to entertain every family of any standing from now until Christmas. I swear that it would quite exhaust me."

"So, you do not care for the social whirl?" asked Novella, attempting to gain some knowledge of her host's romantic life.

"Not really. I prefer the quiet life. My horses, the country and a little hunting are all I require for a happy existence."

"It sounds quite perfect," declared Novella, feeling more and more that he was the kind of person she would like to spend more time with. Then, becoming a little more daring, she broached the subject which she most wanted to discuss.

"And I expect that you are invited to a great many balls being the only eligible bachelor for miles around. I should not wonder that your name is on every young lady's list hereabouts."

Sir Edward laughed long and loud.

"You flatter me, Novella, but you are correct in your assumption that I receive many invitations. However, I have yet to meet a young lady at any of these functions who would pass muster as a future wife – no, she would need to be a rare woman indeed!"

"So have you no thoughts of marriage?" Novella could scarcely believe how forward she was. "Papa always said that love is the reason for living. He and Mama were so happy – "

Novella shocked herself with the way that she had laboured the point.

Blushing to the roots of her hair, she looked away and pretended to be examining a painting on the wall.

"A man always has thoughts – " said Sir Edward, gazing at Novella deeply as she finally made eye contact once more, "but when the time is right, I shall make my choice and you shall be the first to hear of it."

There was an awkward silence as he stared intensely into her eyes. Novella was suddenly overcome with shyness and did not know what had possessed her to ask *such* questions.

'It is quite out of character for me,' she said to herself, as she folded and refolded her napkin, 'after all, it is not as if I am really interested.'

But Novella knew that she was lying to herself. Her interest in Sir Edward was as keen as her appetite had been at dinner. But she was fighting her true feelings.

"Novella?"

"Oh, I am sorry, I was lost in thought."

"But I am being selfish keeping you up. You are no doubt exhausted from the day's trials and tribulations."

"No, not at all," she admitted, "with Mama being so ill, I rarely engage in stimulating conversation with anyone. As my other dealings have all been of a rather distressing nature, it is good for me to have an altogether different kind of discussion."

"Then would you care to join me in the drawing room for coffee?"

"I would love to," replied Novella, clapping her hands together in delight.

As Sir Edward offered her his arm once more, she thrilled at the touch of his hand when it lightly brushed hers as he put her arm under his.

Walking to the drawing room, Novella inhaled the scent of fresh soap and brilliantine. They were the same kind of manly smells that used to emanate from her beloved Papa.

'There is much about him that reminds me of Papa,' she thought, sinking down into a large, silk-covered sofa, 'he talks to me as if I was the most important person in the world at that moment.'

That thought was to keep Novella awake all through the long night that followed. She tossed and turned even though the bed was extremely comfortable.

So when the maid came in the next morning with a tray of tea, Novella felt no more refreshed than when she had first laid her head on the pillow.

"Good morning, my Lady. Sir Edward says that he

will take breakfast with you at nine o'clock. Would you like me to draw you a bath?"

"Thank you, I would like that very much."

Having bathed and put on her blue silk dress once more, Novella brushed her hair and swept it up on her head. She was getting used to dressing herself – in fact, she had become quite adept at inventing new ways to show off her luxuriant dark hair.

'It is such a pity I did not think to put a change of clothing in my bag,' she groaned, looking wistfully at her grubby dress. 'Sir Edward will have tired of seeing me in this.'

But as she entered the dining room, Sir Edward's face lit up.

"Novella! How ravishing you look this morning."

"Thank you," stammered Novella, thinking that, in her opinion, she was far from attractive at that moment.

Novella took the top off her egg and proceeded to eat in silence.

'Why am I being so awkward around Sir Edward this morning?' she puzzled, helping herself to a curl of rich creamy butter. 'Last night I felt completely at ease and now I am like a mumbling schoolgirl!'

She was aware that Sir Edward was still staring at her.

"Novella, do you ever think that one day you might leave Crownley Hall?"

"Goodness, I cannot imagine that," she replied, a little too quickly.

"But should you marry – "

"Then my husband would have to come and live at the Hall."

"That might prove difficult if your stepfather is still at large."

111

"By the time I find a suitable match, I am certain that he will be long dead and buried!"

Sir Edward looked crushed. Novella had the distinct sense that this conversation was leading up to something – but what, she dared not guess.

"So you intend to remain unwed for the time being?"

Novella was not sure how she should answer this question.

In her heart, she now suddenly realised that she loved Sir Edward deeply and utterly, and as she was embarrassed by this revelation, she found it impossible to behave naturally.

"I am sure of nothing whilst Mama lies so ill," she said at last.

"Of course, I can understand that but when, Heaven forbid, she goes to meet her maker, then perhaps you would think of it? It would not be right for a pretty young girl like yourself to be alone in the world."

'What shall I say now?' thought Novella, in a panic. 'I do not feel comfortable with this conversation, but at the same time, I want to find out what he is trying to say.'

"You are correct, I would not care to be alone in the world," she responded eventually, a little stiffly.

"Ah, so it might be possible for you to entertain a proposal at that point?" asked Sir Edward, his greeny-grey eyes burning with love.

Novella's heart began to beat so fast that she feared she would faint. Losing all interest in her breakfast, she put down her spoon and looked up at Sir Edward.

Seeing such naked emotion in his face, she stuttered and failed to say a single word.

"I – I – "

But before she had a chance to answer, there came a

knock at the door.

"Oh, blast," muttered Sir Edward, under his breath. "Come in."

It was his butler.

"Sir Edward, the carriage is ready to take Lady Novella back to her home. When shall I have it brought round to the front of the house?"

"Bring the carriage round in fifteen minutes," ordered Sir Edward.

Novella could see that he was flustered. She wondered what it was that the butler had interrupted.

"But you were saying something," she ventured, as she arose from the table.

"It is of no great importance. We can discuss the matter another time – it will keep. Come, I should not detain you. Your mother will be needing you."

Novella returned to her room and was at a loss as to what to think.

'What was he trying to say to me?' she said again to herself. 'Although he said it was of no importance, he seemed terribly put out that the butler came crashing in at the wrong moment.'

It crossed her mind that he might have been about to ask her to marry him. But she immediately dismissed the notion as fanciful.

'I should not begin to imagine that he cares for me as much as I do him,' she thought, as she waited for someone to come and fetch her bag. 'Besides, I have other more pressing matters. Romance and love will have to wait!'

It was a very reluctant Novella who climbed into the carriage. She did not want to leave but, on the other hand, she was desperate to see her mother.

"You must come again at any time you wish," offered

Sir Edward, as he closed the door behind her. "Please view Tithehurst as a refuge whenever you need one."

"Thank you. Thank you so very much," breathed Novella, leaning out of the carriage window.

"It was my pleasure," he said, reaching out to grasp her fingers.

The carriage started off and still Sir Edward held the tips of her fingers in his.

"I shall call at the Hall very soon, you may be assured of that," he added, a strange look on his face. "Farewell for now."

Novella was close to tears as the carriage made its way down the short drive to the gates. She noticed that Sir Edward walked behind until they had passed through.

"I love him so much!" she cried aloud, not caring if the coach driver heard her.

'But it is simply the wrong time for me to become involved with anyone. I have no idea if he feels the same for me."

In turmoil, she spent the rest of the journey back to Crownley Hall in a state of profound anxiety.

*

Novella felt extremely nervous as the carriage pulled up to the front door of Crownley Hall. While the coach driver unloaded her one bag, the door flew open and Mrs. Armitage came running out.

"My Lady. There you are!"

"Oh, Heavens, Mama, she's not – "

"No my Lady. The nurse has arrived – about fifteen minutes ago. She is with the Countess now."

"What kind of woman is she?"

"Quiet and gentle, my Lady. I think you will be happy with her."

Novella did not hesitate and ran straight upstairs to her mother's room.

Inside, a tall, graceful woman with blonde hair and a pleasant expression was by her bedside.

"You must be Lady Novella," she said, as she wiped the Countess's brow.

"Yes, I am, and you are – ?"

"Nurse Shanks. I was sent by the agency, my Lady, and just in time. Your Mother is gravely ill."

"How ill?"

"I think it will not be long," she whispered, "perhaps a few days, a week or so at most."

Tears sprang into Novella's eyes.

"Thank you, nurse," she replied, staggering away.

'Mama. Oh, Mama,' she cried, as she went back downstairs. 'I cannot believe the time has come.'

As she stood in the hallway, pondering whether or not she wanted to send for Sir Edward, she suddenly heard voices coming from the library.

Tiptoeing towards the door, the sound became louder – and she heard a merry peal of laughter along with the unmistakeable boom of her stepfather's voice.

'Perhaps he has a visitor. Although that would be most strange at this particular time,' she thought.

She stood there for a few moments and could clearly discern that it was a woman's voice that she heard as well as Lord Buckton's.

'I cannot just stand here, I have to investigate.'

Opening the door, nothing could have prepared her for what she found.

"Ah, Novella – " said her stepfather, in a supercilious tone, 'you have deigned to come home at last."

Novella's eyes nearly popped out as she saw a tall overdressed woman in a frothy, pink concoction sitting on the sofa. On her head was a feather so large it could have swept the ceiling, while the face beneath bore the marks of *rouge*.

Horrified, Novella could only stand and stare.

Recovering her senses, she asked in a calm tone,

"So are you not going to introduce me to your visitor, Lord Buckton?"

Her stepfather looked slightly uncomfortable, coughed and then mumbled,

"Novella, this is Mrs. Emma Byesouth. She is a famous actress and acquaintance of mine from London. Our own dear Queen has said that her Lady Macbeth is the best in the world. She has come to stay with us."

Novella could not believe her ears. Had her stepfather taken leave of his senses and all notion of propriety, by bringing his mistress into the house while her Mama was upstairs dying?

She choked back a sob and hurriedly left the library.

"Well, she's a fine sort!" she heard Mrs. Byesouth comment as she ran upstairs.

'I cannot believe how he can be so heartless,' sobbed Novella, opening her bedroom door, 'how can he be so cruel?'

Tears ran down her face and onto her blue silk dress, staining it with dark splotches.

It was then that the full realisation hit her.

'If he seeks to replace Mama before she has died, what will he do to me?'

Never had she felt so alone as she closed the door behind her –

CHAPTER NINE

After a while, Novella pulled herself together and dried her tears. She recognised that she would not be helping her mother by lying on her bed weeping.

Splashing her face with cold water, she reflected upon her current situation.

Now, instead of feeling hopeless, she felt angry again with her stepfather.

'I must carry on in spite of his dreadful behaviour,' she resolved, walking towards her mother's room, 'the least I can do is ensure that Mama has the best of everything while she still draws breath.'

The oil lamp was burning bright as Novella opened the door. Nurse Shanks looked up from her book and moved to rise.

"How is Mama?"

"Very weak, Lady Novella."

"Do – do you think she will last the night?"

Nurse Shanks looked at Novella with a pained expression.

"I am not at all sure, my Lady. It might be for the best if you were to remain here all night."

"Then that is just what I shall do," agreed Novella firmly, as she sank down into a small bedroom chair.

It was soon eleven o'clock and Novella found it difficult to keep awake. So exhausted was she by the past few days that her eyes felt heavy as lead. In fact, since she had returned to Crownley Hall, life had been incredibly hard for her.

'Sometimes I miss the routine of school,' she thought, as she watched her mother's laboured breathing.

There were times when the Countess would appear to cease exhaling and Novella would jump to her feet anxiously, only for her mother's chest to begin to rise and fall once more.

At around midnight, she clearly heard the sound of giggling out on the landing.

Nurse Shanks looked questioningly at her but, too embarrassed to meet the woman's eye, Novella turned her face away – her cheeks hot and flushed.

'This is really too much,' she seethed, not wishing to dwell on whether or not her stepfather and Mrs. Byesouth would occupy separate rooms. 'What on earth must Nurse Shanks think? Probably that she has come into a house of loose morals!'

Long hours passed and she soon fell asleep where she was sitting.

It felt as if she had been asleep no time at all when Nurse Shanks was shaking her awake.

"My Lady, wake up!"

"What is it?" asked Novella sleepily, as she pulled herself upright in the chair.

"Your mother is growing ever worse. I think that the time has come for you to call her husband to her bedside."

"Mama!" cried Novella, with a little choke.

"Ssh! She is in and out of consciousness, my Lady, and can hear you."

Novella arose and went to her mother's side. The Countess was grey in the face and her breath was coming in short bursts.

"My Lady, I urge you – "

Novella quickly made her way from the bedside and out into the hallway. She did not like having to disturb her stepfather, but she knew that she should at least give him the opportunity to redeem himself.

She felt sick at the thought that Mrs. Byesouth might be in her stepfather's room, but she forced herself to knock on the door.

But no reply came.

Knocking again, Novella stood back from the doorway and listened.

'Oh, drat,' she said to herself, but her heart urged her on. Dreadful as he was, surely he would still have some vestige of feeling for her Mama?

Steeling herself this time, Novella pounded on the door even harder.

"Lord Buckton," she screamed, "it is Mama! You must come at once."

This time, she heard a noise and then her stepfather opened the door just a crack, looking dishevelled.

"What is it?" he snapped, "have you no sense of what hour it is?"

"I am sorry, but Mama is dying. Please come to her room."

"Go away, Novella, I am tired. Your mother is probably feigning another one of her 'attacks'. Now, please go and do not bother me again."

"But, Lord Buckton! *She is your wife.*"

Her stepfather's eyes bulged as he sneered through the doorway at her,

"Not for much longer, if you are right."

Then he slammed the door shut.

"You vile, heartless man!" she shouted, hammering on the door once again.

"Come out! Your wife is dying, sir, do you have no feelings?"

But it was in vain. Novella stood there, rapping until her knuckles were raw, but still Lord Buckton did not appear.

Defeated, she walked slowly back to the Countess's room.

But as she entered, the sight that greeted her eyes forced her to cry aloud, her very heart broken in two.

"*No*! Mama!"

For as she walked through the door, she saw that Nurse Shanks was covering her mother's face with a sheet.

"No! No!" cried Novella, sobbing.

"I am so sorry my Lady – but I did not know where Lord Buckton's room was, so I could not come and fetch you. It was very quick and peaceful. She just sighed and went."

Novella was on her knees by her mother's bedside, holding on to that dear hand for the last time.

"Oh, Mama!" she wailed, tears streaming down her face. "You have gone and I was not here with you."

"My Lady, please do not blame yourself. Neither of us could have foreseen what time she would go," soothed the nurse.

"But to die without my being here! I was not there when Papa left us and it is like history repeating itself. I am a terrible, terrible daughter! I should not have left."

Retiring discreetly, the nurse left Novella alone with her mother.

'At least you are now with dear Papa,' whispered

Novella, as she uncovered the Countess's face for a final goodbye. 'You are together, reunited in Heaven. Oh, that sounds like bliss!'

For a single moment, Novella almost envied her mother and wished that she could go with her.

'But I must go on,' she urged herself resolutely, 'Crownley Hall needs me.'

*

As soon as morning broke, there was much activity in the Hall. After Nurse Shanks had alerted Mrs. Armitage, first Lily and then Charles got up in the cold and the dark.

Charles saddled up Salamander and with Novella's permission, rode as fast as he could to Doctor Jones.

Novella stayed in her mother's room until the doctor arrived.

As she waited, she thought constantly of Sir Edward. Should she send word to him? But, no, she decided. It was best left alone.

'Who will care for me now?' she asked, as she looked at her mother's peaceful face. 'I am now all alone in the world.'

She thought of Sir Edward's expression as they had parted on the previous day and something, deep down, told her that she was not on her own.

Even so, she refused to believe it.

'I should not begin to rely upon him,' she thought, as she heard the sound of a carriage pulling up outside, 'that would be most unwise.'

Equally she found it hard to forget about him.

Rushing to the window, she saw Charles dismounting from Salamander and then helping Doctor Jones out of his carriage.

Doctor Jones had a very distressed air as he walked

into the hallway of Crownley Hall.

"It seems like only yesterday I was here to attend to your dear Papa." he said, as he allowed Novella to lead him upstairs to where the Countess was lying.

"I shall let you proceed unhindered," said Novella, as she opened the bedroom door for him.

"Then I will do what is necessary and I shall leave the certificate with Mrs. Armitage, if that is acceptable?"

"Yes, please do."

As she walked along the landing, she saw her stepfather standing down in the hallway. He was wearing his outdoor clothes and had obviously just arrived back home. Novella was unaware that he had left Crownley Hall and thought that he must have taken Mrs. Byesouth to the station very early that morning without anyone noticing.

'The cheek of the man,' she scowled, as she glared at him.

Catching sight of her, Lord Buckton came towards her up the stairs.

"Well?" he said, no hint of emotion on his face.

"Mama died this morning, sir," she replied, stiffly.

"More expense," he answered, with a shrug of his shoulders.

It was more than Novella could bear. She was so tired she could hardly stand and so very full of anger at his behaviour.

She flew at him, her fists pummelling his dirt-stained riding habit.

"You beast! You are not fit to set foot inside Crownley Hall, let alone take it over as if it was your own. Mama died but a few hours ago and all you can think of is how much money her funeral will cost! Do you have no finer feelings? How dare you! *How dare you!*"

But Lord Buckton simply looked at Novella and laughed.

"Control yourself, my dear," he said, dismissively, "you are now a very rich young woman, isn't that enough for you?"

"For you it is always about money. You are an excuse for a human being. You deceived Mama into marrying you in the hope of receiving a fortune – well, I can tell you, Lord Buckton, that neither Crownley Hall nor Mama's money will come to you! Papa left a will stating that everything comes to me. Do you hear?"

Never before had Novella behaved in such a fashion – her eyes were flashing and her voice was loud and firm.

In the midst of all this, Mrs. Byesouth appeared at the top of the staircase – she had not left the house and looked as if she had only just dressed herself.

"And as for you bringing this – this immoral character into the house. Words defy me! You have defiled Mama's memory by behaving in an improper fashion with her.

"And you, Mrs. Byesouth, you have no shame if you are happy to jump into a dead woman's shoes, before she is even cold."

Mrs. Byesouth reddened and looked as if she wished the ground would swallow her up.

Trying to maintain as dignified a stance as was possible given the circumstances, she pulled herself up to her full height and quietly said,

"I think it would be best if I left," before turning round and going back upstairs.

That was all Lord Buckton required to provoke one of his rages.

He spun round on his heel and slapped Novella hard around the face. She gulped as she reeled from both the blow and the shock.

"Are you happy with yourself now?" he shouted, "you have grossly insulted Mrs. Byesouth."

"And you are callous and heartless," retorted Novella, holding her face. She tried not to cry, even though the blow had brought tears to her eyes. She did all she could not let him see how hurt she was.

Lord Buckton lowered his voice to almost a whisper,

"Get back upstairs and I will deal with you later."

Novella began to shake – he was far more terrifying when he was quietly threatening than when he shouted at her.

"Anything to not be in your vile presence!" she replied, defiantly tossing back her head. She was trying hard not to show how very shaken she was by his blow. If he saw how upset she was – then he would have won.

Closing her bedroom door, she let herself cry. Hot tears splashed down her face as she undressed and then lay on the bed. Sobbing into the pillow, the full weight of her grief overtook her.

'Oh, Mama. I miss you so much already. I feel as if I cannot bear to be in this house while that awful man is here. But what choice do I have? I am so alone – who is there to take care of me now?'

As she cried herself to sleep, Novella knew that there was someone who cared for her – if only she dared to believe it to be true –

*

A few hours later, Novella awoke. Lily had been in and left her a luncheon tray on the dressing table with a cold-beef sandwich and a glass of milk.

Novella looked at it sleepily and felt sick at the thought of food in her stomach. She could not face the milk.

'I would like something less cloying,' she thought,

rising, her mouth so dry her tongue was almost sticking to it. 'I will go and see what else Mrs. Armitage has in the pantry – I also should like to see the death certificate that Doctor Jones left earlier.'

So it was with some surprise that Novella descended the stairs just in time to see a small party of men being led into the library. In her sleepy state, she wondered who they might be.

"Many condolences, my Lady" said a tall gentleman wearing a top hat. "She was a fine lady."

Novella looked blankly at the stranger.

"I am sorry, have we met before? I do apologise if so, but understandably, I am not quite myself."

"No, my Lady, I have not had that pleasure. But it is a fine house you have here. Well worth the asking price."

Novella stared at him in horror.

"I do beg your pardon?" she said, but the man had disappeared to catch up the rest of the group.

Just then, Mrs. Armitage appeared.

"Ah, my Lady," she began.

"Mrs. Armitage," interrupted Novella, "who are these strange people wandering around? Surely they have not come to see Mama's lying in?"

"Oh, no, my Lady. That would not be possible at any rate, seeing as how her Ladyship's body has already been taken to the undertakers."

"But – but, how can that be when we have not had the lying in? People from the estate and the village will want to say goodbye to her."

"Sorry, my Lady. Lord Buckton ordered it. He thought it best if people went there rather than troop around the Hall disturbing us all."

Novella was dumbstruck. Did her wishes count for

nothing?

She suddenly felt an overwhelming urge for some fresh air. The day was a fine one and it seemed as if being inside the walls of the Hall was becoming oppressive to her.

Walking out onto the drive, Novella saw Charles coming towards her. She noted, with tenderness, that he was already wearing a black armband.

"My Lady," he said in a shaky voice, "her Ladyship is in Heaven now at last with his Lordship."

"That is true, Charles, and I am deeply touched by your grief."

"Well, I was with her Ladyship for many years, my Lady. Grew up working for 'er."

"How is Salamander?"

"He knows summat is up, does the old boy. Sensitive creatures – horses."

"I would dearly like to see him, is he in his stable?"

"Yes, my Lady."

"Then let us go and visit him."

Novella thought that stroking Salamander's silky mane and feeling his warmth would make her feel better. Her step felt lighter as she entered the stables.

Sensing that she was near, Salamander let out a whinny of delight.

"Salamander, darling!" she cried, running to him and throwing her arms around his neck.

As she petted him, she could not help but cry.

"I feel as if you are my only friend," she whispered, hugging his neck.

But no sooner had she spoke, than she thought of Sir Edward and the offer he had made to her of his house always being available to her as a sanctuary.

Without thinking twice, she called to Charles,

"Charles. Saddle up Salamander for me."

"But you are not wearing your riding habit."

"I don't care. Please make him ready for me."

It did not take Charles long to saddle up Salamander and, without a backward glance, Novella mounted him and rode off.

'I need to be away from the Hall – never before have I felt a stranger in my own home,' she thought, as she rode off into the warm afternoon sunshine towards Tithehurst.

*

By the time she arrived, she was crying and her hair was flowing loose around her shoulders.

Sir Edward was about to go out and was climbing into his carriage when Novella rode through the gates looking dishevelled.

"Novella!" he shouted, running towards her, "what on earth – ?"

"Oh, Edward," she sobbed, almost fainting whilst still seated on Salamander.

"Quick! You, ostler, take the horse and I will see to her Ladyship."

In a second, Sir Edward had carried Novella, still in a swoon, from her horse and had brought her inside the house.

"Mama – she is dead!" sobbed Novella, as she clung to his neck.

"Coachman, take the carriage back to the stables. I am no longer going out."

"Yes, sir."

Inside the house, Sir Edward carried Novella into the airy drawing room and laid her down on the sofa.

"Now, I want to know everything that has happened,"

coaxed Sir Edward, pouring a small glass of brandy.

And so, Novella told him the whole sorry tale – from discovering Mrs. Byesouth in the Hall to the awful gangs of people picking over the Hall.

"But that is dreadful!" exclaimed Sir Edward, when she admitted that Lord Buckton had struck her. "The man is worse than an animal."

"I may have provoked him, but Edward, I was so angry. Mama not yet cold and already he has his fancy woman installed and people milling around the Hall for Heaven knows what reason."

"You must stay here tonight, of course. I meant what I said that you must treat this house as your place of retreat."

Novella looked up him, gratefully.

"I cannot tell you how much that means to me."

There was a long silence as their eyes met and Novella was suddenly filled with a strange emotion. Looking away, she sipped at the brandy and wrapped herself in the blanket. Although it was warm outside, she was shivering from shock and exhaustion.

"Who is arranging the funeral?" asked Sir Edward, after a while.

"I should suppose that would be my responsibility," sighed Novella, "I cannot see that my stepfather would be bothered."

"Then you must allow me to help, of course."

"That would be wonderful," she replied, her heart swelling with emotion.

"And you will need to visit your solicitors, naturally."

"Yes, you are right. If, as I believe, my stepfather is attempting to sell the Hall out from beneath me, I will need to make sure that does not happen."

"We should try and see them as soon as possible. Do

you feel capable of making the trip today? There are still a few hours left before their office shuts."

Novella looked down at her dress in dismay. It was rumpled and stained from her journey on Salamander.

"I should not say this, but you look so beautiful," Sir Edward murmured, taking her by the hand and leading her outside.

'Could he have feelings for me?' thought Novella as they sat close in the carriage. 'Perhaps he is trying to be of comfort and does not have any romantic inclinations towards me.'

All the way into Stockington he held on to her hand causing Novella to become increasingly emotional. She was uncertain if it was just a matter of her feelings running riot due to her recent bereavement or whether there was more to it?

Sir Edward guided her through the awful experience of the undertakers – Novella found it very difficult when she came to view her beloved Mama's body – and then, with the details of the funeral settled, they proceeded to the offices of Rumbold and Humbert.

Mr. Humbert Senior was in court that day, so Mr. Rumbold attended her.

He opened up the vast sheet of parchment in front of him.

"As soon as I heard the news this morning about your mother, I made ready with the necessary documentation. As I believe my colleague, Mr. Humbert Senior has told you, everything now comes to you in spite of the Countess's recent marriage."

"Is that not contrary to the law of the land?" put in Sir Edward.

"It is a most unusual case, Sir Edward, and a very interesting one. However, the Earl was very thorough with his original will and although usually a woman gives up her rights to her property upon marriage, there was a special dispensation on this particular occasion."

"So Lady Novella will inherit everything?"

"Indeed she will."

"I believe that my stepfather is currently trying to sell the Hall," announced Novella, wearily.

"It is not his to sell, my Lady," replied Mr Rumbold. "However, I am afraid that we are already in receipt of a letter from Lord Buckton's solicitor contesting your late father's will."

"Already," exclaimed Novella, alarmed, "but Mama only died this morning. He must have put this into motion some weeks ago. This is outrageous!"

"I would tend to agree with you, my Lady. But in my long years in this profession, I have seen this kind of thing before. Greed is a great motivator. He has also sought to gain access to your bank account – there is a letter about that as well."

"I expected as much. Mr. Longridge had warned me."

"Tell me, my Lady, as you are so worried about what your stepfather may do next, have you had the opportunity to check in the secret place for her Ladyship's jewels?"

"Secret place?" asked Novella, her eyes widening.

"Yes, your father was a wise man – he was also mindful of the fact that your mother would often be left alone in the house overnight. He was worried that thieves would take advantage of his frequent absences and would rob her. So, he commissioned a craftsman to build a secret place in her bed for her valuables. I believe that both you and your father had identical beds?"

"Yes, they are very ornate with lots of carvings," replied Novella, growing more excited by the second. "I loved the fact that I had one just like theirs – especially when I small. I was so relieved when I returned to Crownley Hall to find that my bed had been moved to my new room."

"Ah, yes. Your stepfather took over your old room, did he not?"

"How did you know?"

"Oh, village gossip, my Lady."

Novella was shocked. Once more she was mortified that her stepfather had made the family the subject of tittle-tattle, and it made her utterly embarrassed to be associated with him.

"In any eventuality, my Lady, you should search in the carvings above the bed. There you will find a catch and inside a secret compartment holding your mother's valuables."

"I had thought that my stepfather had sold them all off."

"Some things may have indeed been sold, but I would wager that there will be a great deal left for you."

As it was growing late, Novella thanked the gentleman and rose to leave. Sir Edward jumped up from his seat and took her arm in his.

"Good luck Lady Novella and remember the law is on your side," said Mr. Rumbold as she left the office.

"Oh, I am so relieved," she cried, as they climbed back into Sir Edward's carriage, "and what exciting news about the hiding place!"

"But you are not planning on returning back to Crownley Hall tonight, surely?" asked Sir Edward, a worried look marring his handsome features.

"I had not thought to stay at Tithehurst – " replied Novella, her eyes cast downwards modestly.

"I insist. You cannot go home this evening and face

your stepfather. Novella, you have endured more than most and you need a respite from your trauma. Going back tonight will only make you unhappy. Return tomorrow after a refreshing night's sleep. I am sure that Jean-Charles will provide us with a delicious dinner – that is, if you are hungry?"

"I was not earlier today but do you know, I am now famished," exclaimed Novella, cheering up immensely.

And with that, she looked into Sir Edward's eyes and saw that his expression was so tender that it quite took her breath away.

*

Novella was treated as a special guest that evening.

Feeling refreshed, Novella walked slowly downstairs to dinner.

Sir Edward was waiting for her in the dining room and they enjoyed a wonderful meal together.

Jean-Charles excelled himself, serving a wonderful *bisque d' homard*, followed by veal cutlets in the French style. Pudding was a *chartreuse* of strawberries.

"That was delicious. Jean-Charles is a superb cook and I am most envious," sighed Novella, pleasantly full.

"I am very lucky, I agree," said Sir Edward, "now let us retire to the drawing room for coffee and brandy."

Taking Novella's arm, the pair walked the short distance to the adjoining room. The atmosphere was so calm – so unlike that of Crownley Hall.

For Novella, the Hall had become less of a home with each day that Lord Buckton inhabited it.

Sir Edward's butler brought in the brandy and they sat in opposite chairs by the fireplace.

"What will you do, Novella? You are welcome to stay as long as you like at Tithehurst, but you will have to go home eventually."

Novella hung her head and she could feel the tears pricking her eyes at the very thought.

"I do not know, Edward. The Hall is not a home to me at present but I have such strong ties to it. My main problem lies in trying to get Lord Buckton out."

She could not contain herself. The thought of such a task filled her with dismay and made her feel quite helpless.

Hot tears ran down her cheeks and into her glass of brandy.

"Novella, dearest," urged Sir Edward, leaving his chair and kneeling at her feet. "Please do not upset yourself."

"I am sorry, it is just that I feel so alone and I do not know what will become of me and Crownley Hall. It is such a huge responsibility – I am not sure I can cope with it."

"But you are not alone, Novella, you have friends around you who care very deeply for you."

"It does not feel that way."

"Then, look in front of your eyes. Oh, Novella! I cannot keep my feelings to myself a moment longer."

Taking her hand gently in his, Sir Edward kissed it tenderly before continuing,

"I realise that this may not be the best possible time to speak of such things, but you must know that there is someone who would lay down his life for you."

Looking up into his eyes, Novella could hardly believe her ears. Her heart beat so fast that she could not breathe and she waited for his next words.

"Yes, Novella, I have loved you from the very first moment I set eyes upon you."

"Oh, *Edward*." breathed Novella, as he rose and took her into his arms.

"It is true. I speak my heart to you now. God is my witness. I cannot bear to see you in such distress so even though I know my timing is dreadful, I need you to know that you are not alone. I love you, *I love you*. And I want you to know it now!"

"Edward," she murmured, her eyes closing in ecstasy.

Sir Edward leaned towards her, kissing first her hair and then her eyes and lastly, her lips.

'I am so happy I swear I will burst,' thought Novella, as she emerged from a long and tender kiss.

"Darling," continued Sir Edward, holding her tight and showering her with tiny kisses, "you need never fear again for I am here beside you to be your rock, your strength.

"Do not worry about Lord Buckton, for together we will outwit him and claim Crownley Hall as yours and yours alone. *I love you and want to marry you*."

Novella gasped, her heart bursting with the love that comes only from above.

The world seemed to stand still as she nestled into his arms, safe and free from harm.

"Dearest Edward," she whispered, feeling the warmth of him against her cheek.

"Novella, dearest love, would you, once your period of mourning is over, consider becoming my wife?"

Sir Edward looked deep into her eyes and waited for her answer –

CHAPTER TEN

Novella looked at Sir Edward – her head reeling from what she had just heard him say.

She desperately wanted to answer him, but no sound came out of her mouth.

With so many mixed emotions taking hold of her, she did not know how to reply.

Sir Edward, sensing her discomfiture, pulled back from her.

His face fell and his eyes looked wistful as he said,

"I do not expect your answer now – I have been a trifle hasty. I can see that."

Novella suddenly feared that she would lose him and everything that was good and hopeful in her life.

Grasping his shoulders, she looked up at him, her eyes full of love and sincerity.

"No, no!" she cried, feeling that happiness was about to slip from her fingers, "I love you too. I *will* become your wife. No matter what happens, this I promise you!"

Almost bursting with joy, she felt Sir Edward's arms enfold her as he drew her close once more and kissed her tenderly on the lips.

Novella now knew what it was to love and be loved and it filled her mind, her body and her soul with such ecstasy that she felt as if she was touching Heaven itself.

"Darling, what will you do now?" asked Sir Edward as they stood in an embrace by the fireplace.

"I should like to stay here tonight, but I am afraid I simply must return to the Hall tomorrow morning. I do not trust my stepfather one inch."

"You must allow me to accompany you."

"No, I have to do this on my own. I can send word for you if I need you. But there are family matters that need to be settled and it would not be right for you to witness them."

"Novella, my precious, I understand, but equally you must know that I am beside you every step of the way."

"And I thank you for that, Edward, my dearest. But my stepfather's temper is short at the best of times and I do not wish you to become involved."

"Novella, whatever problems you have are mine too," he pleaded.

Novella looked up at him, his beautiful eyes so full of love for her – could she have imagined a finer man as her fiancé?

"Edward, I have wanted to say that I loved you for a long time," she confessed, nestling in his arms, so safe and secure.

"I could not read what you were thinking," replied Sir Edward, "you seemed so distant at times and you are so young too. Lord Buckton is a strong-willed man. I am surprised that he did not have a suitable match ready for you."

"No, I was worth more to him unmarried," responded Novella bitterly, "he has the notion that he will be able to get his hands on my money now that Mama has died. He would not want to risk a rival for the inheritance entering the picture."

"Novella, there is something else I wish to say to you that is most important," said Sir Edward, leading her back to her fireside chair.

"What is that, my dearest?"

"You do know, do you not, that I am not in the slightest bit interested in your assets? I have a large, personal fortune thanks to my father's will and I have no designs on being the Lord of Crownley Hall."

"Darling, I know that!" cried Novella, squeezing his hand.

"Now, I think it is time that you retired, you are looking a little fatigued. It has been a most difficult day for you."

"Yes, you are right," sighed Novella, for in spite of all the excitement she felt at her new love, she was very very tired.

"Your room will be ready for you – now go – I will see you in the morning."

He kissed her eyes gently and rang for the maid so that she could show Novella upstairs.

Sir Edward walked as far as the landing with Novella and then kissed her once more.

"Goodnight, my darling one," he whispered, "until tomorrow – sleep well."

"And you too," murmured Novella before moving towards her room.

"And do not forget – you are no longer on your own, you have me by your side and now your stepfather has me to contend with as well."

Novella smiled to herself still unable to believe how fortunate she was to have found love with a man like Edward.

'Papa and Mama would have adored him,' she

thought, as she watched the maid turning back the bed and making sure that there was enough water in the jug.

'I do so hope that they are looking down on us and giving us their blessing.'

And that thought comforted her immensely.

*

Although excited, Novella quickly fell asleep and, before she knew it, the maid was pulling back the curtains and letting in a stream of brilliant sunshine.

Rubbing her eyes, Novella wondered if she had indeed dreamt everything that had happened the previous evening. After such a hideous run of luck, it all seemed too good to be true.

But as soon as she entered the dining room for breakfast and saw Sir Edward, so anxious and so nervous, she knew that she had not imagined it.

Running towards her, he took her hand and kissed it many times over.

"My darling, how did you sleep?"

As he gazed at her, loving and attentive, Novella felt overwhelmed.

"I was asleep as soon as my head touched the pillow," she said, not letting his hand go. "And now, I am quite hungry."

"Jean-Charles has made some kedgeree, would you care for some?"

"That sounds wonderful, thank you."

Novella seated herself at the table as Sir Edward took it upon himself to pile up a plate from the buffet for her. His butler stood by, with an amused look on his face at having been temporarily relieved of his duties.

"What will you do this morning?" asked Sir Edward looking concerned.

"I must return to the Hall as soon as I have eaten," replied Novella, savouring the tasty dish, "I want to search for that secret hiding place that Mr. Rumbold told us about. I feel sure that Lord Buckton will have ransacked the place already searching for what remains of Mama's jewels."

"And you are still certain that you wish to return alone?"

Novella felt torn. It was a most attractive offer – for she knew that facing her stepfather again would be difficult – but she knew she had to face him on her own.

"Yes," she answered after a long pause, "it cannot be any other way."

"I will be at your immediate disposal should you require me," offered Sir Edward.

Novella longed to cry out 'Yes! Yes. Come with me,' but she knew that would only make what she needed to do more difficult. She had no wish to draw attention to herself in her hunt for the secret hiding place.

"We should also keep the news of our engagement a secret until after the funeral," murmured Novella, aware that it was bound to cause a sensation in any eventuality.

But she did not care for convention – as soon as her Mama's funeral had taken place, she would have no compunction in making the announcement.

"I agree," said Sir Edward, rising from the breakfast table. "Now, I will have the carriage made ready for you."

Novella left to put her few things into an old tapestry bag that had belonged to Sir Edward's sister and then steeled herself for the return journey home.

Downstairs, the carriage was ready and Sir Edward's coachman was seated on the box, holding the reins of a fine pair of black horses.

"I think it would be best if I kept Salamander stabled

here until such time as it is safe for him to return," Sir Edward told her as they embraced for one last time. "And you are to send word to me the instant you require me. Send Ned on Bluebell – she can still kick up the turf like a young mare."

Novella smiled – how he loved the horses as much as she did. It made her adore him all the more.

Climbing up into the carriage, she settled down with a feeling of apprehension. In truth, she did not wish to return home at all – but she had important discoveries to make.

"I will keep Salamander in the top field out of the way of prying eyes," promised Sir Edward, as he held her hand through the carriage window. "That way, Lord Buckton cannot come and take him by force."

"Thank you so much, my dearest. If I lost Salamander again after losing Mama, I do not know how I would cope. It is only you and he that keep me going."

*

And so Novella returned to Crownley Hall.

She was so nervous as she walked through the front door that she felt quite sick, but she was relieved and somewhat surprised to find that her stepfather was not at home.

As she walked around the Hall, she could see that more items had disappeared.

Returning to her room, it felt strange and empty.

She was just about to start climbing up onto her bed to search for the hidden place, when Mrs. Armitage entered without knocking.

'Bother,' she thought, as she hastily climbed down. The last thing she wanted was for Mrs. Armitage's curiosity to be aroused.

"Ah, my Lady – you have returned at last. I am glad

to see you safe and sound."

"I stayed with a friend – I am afraid that I needed to get away from the cares of the Hall for a while."

"You have made the funeral arrangements, I trust?"

"Has my stepfather been asking?"

"No, my Lady, he is in London on business. It is just that there have been many callers making enquiries."

"I shall send out the cards this afternoon," said Novella with a sigh, "I believe there are some black-bordered cards in Mama's room left over from Papa's funeral. There is not time to have more printed – they are blank and will have to suffice."

"Shall I clean and press your best mourning clothes?" asked Mrs. Armitage.

Novella gave her a look – how did she know that she had them? She must have been rummaging around in her wardrobe during her absence!

"Thank you, Mrs. Armitage. The crepe on the bodice of my best dress may need replacing. Can I ask you to attend to it?"

"Of course, my Lady."

"And I should like another veil ordered, can you send for one from Peter Robinson's in London?"

"Yes, my Lady. Will that be all?"

"Yes, thank you," replied Novella.

But even so, Mrs. Armitage lingered for a moment longer, her eyes darting around the bed to see if she could fathom what Novella was up to.

"*Thank you*, Mrs. Armitage!" repeated Novella, dismissing her. She was eager for the housekeeper to leave so that she could press on with her plans.

*

For the next few days, such was the amount that required Novella's attention, that finding the secret cache had to take second place.

There was so much to organise. She had the cards to write, announcing the day and time of the Countess's funeral. Then there were the numerous trips to the undertakers to take locks of hair from her Mama to make into memorial jewellery – and next the visit to the jewellers to have the pendant made.

Novella had no wish for a death mask to be fashioned and there was the matter of ensuring that every window in Crownley Hall was correctly shuttered.

Novella lived and breathed mourning and funerals until the day itself.

There had been mutterings in the village about the prolonged absence of Lord Buckton, but nobody was really very shocked.

As Novella sorted through her mother's effects, she was utterly taken over by bouts of weeping. Mama's clothes still smelled of the cologne that she used to wear on occasions, mingled with the lavender bags that kept the moths at bay.

She broke down completely when she found her Mama's wedding dress. She sobbed into the soft silk of the skirt whilst kneeling in front of the wardrobe.

'Oh, Mama! I wish you were here. I can only hope that you are able to see me from Heaven and that you know how I have found true love amidst all this sorrow.'

In a way, Novella was grateful that her stepfather did not put in an appearance at the Hall but remained in London. At least it gave her plenty of time to do what was necessary.

It was obvious to her that Lord Buckton had indeed been through her mother's things – there were drawers with rumpled contents instead of being neatly folded and she found empty hat boxes and cases that had been forced open.

But Novella still did not have the chance to search the bed as each time she attempted it, as if by magic, Mrs. Armitage appeared. It was as if she had been told to keep a close eye on her to see if she would reveal where the really important, saleable items were.

Eventually, Novella decided that it would be best if she waited until after the funeral – with so many comings and goings at the Hall, she really did not have time for a prolonged search.

And so, the day of the funeral eventually dawned.

Sir Edward came to the Hall first thing in the morning and Novella could not help but admire how smart he looked in his black mourning suit.

'He is more handsome than ever,' she said to herself, as he stayed by her side while the mourners gathered in front of the Hall.

At eleven o'clock, the hearse arrived. It was a glass carriage pulled by six black horses with plumes on their heads.

Novella had been quite composed until the moment that she saw her Mama's coffin inside the vehicle and then she began to cry profusely.

Sir Edward took her arm and guided her towards his carriage that had been especially liveried in black for the occasion. Even his coachman was wearing a black overcoat instead of his usual dark green and gold.

The funeral procession wound its slow way to the local Church and Novella was stunned to see that practically everyone in the village had turned out.

"I did not think it was possible that Mama was so loved," she said to Sir Edward as they climbed down from the carriage.

Later, as they stood around the grave, there were mutterings from within the crowd remarking upon Lord Buckton's absence. Although it was outrageous that he was not present, Novella was secretly pleased.

She had not wanted her stepfather to be by her side throughout the service and around the grave – she was pleased that it was Sir Edward who held her arm and comforted her.

'Goodbye, dearest Mama,' whispered Novella, as she took a handful of dirt from the box and threw it into the open grave, 'rest easy with Papa and I will see you one day again.'

Leading her towards his carriage, Sir Edward suddenly turned to her,

"Do you wish me to come back to the Hall with you?" he asked gently.

"No, I would like to be alone and to rest," she replied, feeling quite exhausted. The whole weight of everything that had happened lay heavy upon her.

"Then you must take my carriage. I will go with Mr. Longridge in his."

Mr. Hubert Longridge had indeed attended the service and could be seen with tears in his eyes throughout. In fact, Novella could not think of a single friend or tradesman who had ever dealt with the family who had not put in an appearance.

Reluctantly, Sir Edward saw Novella to his carriage and then took her hand briefly – he knew it would not be right to give her a kiss with so many people watching.

"Darling, I wish I could cover your face with kisses, but it would not be seemly. Please look after yourself and send for me immediately should you need me."

"I will, my love," she replied, gratefully, as the carriage began to pull away.

Novella's heart was in her mouth as she approached the Hall. Travelling down the long drive, she could see that her stepfather had returned and that he appeared to be accompanied by a rough-looking man.

As they drew up outside the front door, Lord Buckton turned to greet her.

"Ah, Novella," he called, "I am so sorry that I could not attend your Mama's funeral, I have only just returned from London."

Stepping onto the drive, Novella gave the man next to him a long look. She waited for her stepfather to introduce them.

It was then that she noticed that all the closed shutters in the house had been reopened.

After a giving a nervous cough, Lord Buckton spoke,

"Let us go inside, my dear," he said, almost kindly, "I want you to meet Mr. Preston – he is waiting inside and is most anxious to speak with you."

Fear sprang up at once in Novella's bosom. The man that Lord Buckton was speaking to when she arrived looked alarmingly like a builder.

She could see that his hands were rough from hard work and he had the complexion of a man who spent a great deal of time outdoors.

"What matter does he wish to discuss with me?" she asked in a cool tone.

"I think that it is best if we go indoors and talk there," insisted her stepfather, beginning to look irritated.

"Very well."

Lord Buckton took her into the library, by which time Novella's heart was beating fast. She had just been through one dreadful experience and now it seemed that she was about to have another.

What was more, her stepfather's avuncular air was not the least bit in character and that alone was enough to worry her.

"Sit down, my dear."

Lord Buckton offered her a comfortable chair and, reluctantly, Novella sank down into it.

As she did so, she noticed that a second man was in the library already. She had not noticed him at first – although Heaven only knows how she did not, for he was dressed in a loud-checked overcoat with a pink silk waistcoat. Not quite smart enough to be a dandy, but Novella immediately began to suspect that something was afoot.

She glared at the man, feeling that he was intruding upon her grief. The man shifted in his chair by the window, obviously uncomfortable.

"My dear, this is Mr. Preston. He and his colleague have come to see what needs doing to Crownley Hall. I have it in mind to put the estate up for sale now that your Mama has gone. Now, if you will just be so kind as to sign this paper, we can conclude our business and Mr. Preston can be on his way."

Novella was so angry that she was shaking.

'How dare he! It is not his to sell,' she thought, but was unable to speak.

"Mr. Preston has made me a very generous offer for the Hall and I have decided to take it."

"Enough!" shouted Novella, standing up, her eyes blazing. "May I remind you that it is not yours to sell? *Crownley Hall is now mine.* You know the terms of Papa's will and *I* inherit everything upon Mama's death – not *you!*"

"You will have to excuse Lady Novella," remarked Lord Buckton, in a patronising tone to Mr. Preston, "she buried her mother this morning."

"How dare you try and sell Crownley Hall from over my head!" she continued, standing her ground, "Mama is barely in her grave!"

Mr. Preston turned red and looked down at his highly polished shoes.

"Er-hem, I am sorry, my Lady, but there seems to have been a misunderstanding. I was given to believe that it was Lord Buckton's property to sell and of course, if it is not, then I do not wish to become embroiled in any family quarrels –"

He rose to leave, taking his hat with him.

"And I certainly did not realise it was the day of your mother's funeral else I would not have even set foot inside the house. Please forgive the intrusion. Lord Buckton, I am sorry, but we no longer have a deal."

With a short bow, the embarrassed Mr. Preston quickly left the room.

As he shut the door behind him, Novella turned to face her stepfather. She could see that he was beside himself with rage – his face was purple and his breath was coming in short noisy bursts.

"You – will – pay – for this," he spluttered, grabbing her by the arm so hard that his fingernails bit through the thin silk of her dress.

Without hesitating, he dragged her out of the library and up the stairs to her room. Throwing her on to the bed, he strode back to the door and, with a flourish, took the key from the lock.

"You will stay here until I see fit to let you out. When you have cooled down, we will talk about this matter again. I will sell Crownley Hall. *It is mine by right!*"

With that, he locked the door behind him.

'Oh, why didn't I hide the key as I have been doing of

late?' wept Novella.

But she had been so preoccupied with thoughts of her mother's funeral that it had slipped her mind. And now, she was incarcerated once more.

'What can I do? What *can* I do?' she asked herself repeatedly, weeping all the while. Never had Novella felt so hopeless.

'As if it were not enough that today is the day of Mama's funeral, I am now a prisoner in my own home.'

Looking up at the ceiling, Novella tried to fathom out what to do. She was certain that Charles would still be in the village, drinking to her mother's memory with the rest of the stable boys and, without him, she had no chance of sending for Sir Edward.

'Why, oh, why did I send him away?' she cried, pummelling the bed covers. 'I need him now more than ever. I was so foolish.'

But there was nothing she could do and Novella realised that.

Her eyes scanned the room until she was looking straight overhead up at her bedhead with its intricate carvings of acorns and leaves.

'The hiding place,' she suddenly remembered, 'and if there was one in Mama's bed and all the beds were made at the same time, then perhaps there is one in mine.'

Excitedly, she stood on tiptoe and began to pull at various carvings.

'Oh, goodness,' she wondered, her arms aching with the effort, 'perhaps there is not the same feature on my bed.'

But just then, she found what felt like a small catch underneath one of the leaves. Holding her breath, she pushed it to one side and, to her amazement, a small door opened.

'Now, if I can stretch up and feel inside – ' she urged herself, straining her muscles till they started shaking.

Then her hand closed around something cold and metallic. Pulling it out, bit-by-bit, she gasped as there in her hand was a key!

'This looks just like the one for my bedroom door,' she cried, before rushing over to the door to try it.

Sure enough, it fitted.

'I must not waste any more time, I must run to Mama's room and see if I can find hers.'

Novella's heart was beating so loud that she was sure that it could be heard downstairs, but she stood and waited to make certain that no one was around.

Satisfied that her stepfather had gone out, she re-locked her bedroom door and tucked the key into the sash of her dress.

'Thank Heavens I had Mrs. Armitage sew a small pocket in it for handkerchiefs,' she thought, as she made her way to her mother's room.

It was cold and dark inside. Closing the door carefully behind her, she took that key out of the lock so that she would not find herself imprisoned should someone surprise her.

Looking up at the carved bedhead, Novella could hardly wait to start her search. Carefully, she climbed up on to the huge bed and began to feel around the acorns. Almost in the same place as she had found the catch on her own bedhead, there, underneath a leaf was the very same.

Moving it to one side, she held her breath as she reached up. Feeling inside the hole, her fingers grasped what felt like a necklace. Pulling it out, Novella let out a stifled scream as there, sparkling in her hand, was a string of emeralds!

'It is grandmother's!' she cried. 'I cannot believe that Lord Buckton did not get his hands on it. I wonder what else is inside?'

Novella held her breath as she stood on the pillow and delved deeper inside the hollow. Within seconds, she had pulled out a diamond tiara and a couple of rings.

She could not help herself – tears of joy began to course down her face.

'Mama! Oh, clever Mama. These are all her most precious pieces of jewellery – the jewels that my stepfather managed to find were not the very best of her collection. Oh, Mama, I am so pleased.'

She decided to stand on yet one more pillow to reach right into the back of the hollow. As she did, her fingers brushed against something cold and hard.

'What is this? Could it be another key for the bedroom?' she wondered.

Stretching in so far that her arm ached, Novella's fingers just about hooked around the item. Breathing out, she pulled it from its hiding place and it fell onto the bed heavily, bringing a key on a blue ribbon with it.

Novella stood and looked at what had fallen out – utter horror on her face.

'A pistol' she whispered, 'what was Mama doing with a pistol in her bed? And this must be the key to her bedroom.'

She held up the pistol by its blue ribbon. It was then that she remembered that her mother had once confided in her that her father had made her sleep with a pistol under her pillow whenever he went away for long periods of time.

'Of course. Papa was always worried that robbers would break into the house when he was away and so he made sure that Mama could protect herself. She must have put it in here out of harm's way.'

Voices downstairs in the hallway alerted Novella to the fact that there were people around.

Quickly, she pulled the pillowcase off the pillow and began to stuff the jewels into it.

'I must get back to my room as soon as possible,' she thought.

But no sooner had she put the last piece into the pillowcase when her stepfather stormed into the room with an Officer of the law close behind.

"Ah, just as I thought," he snarled. "As you can see, Officer, my stepdaughter is not only a cheat who would do me out of my legal rights, but she is a thief. Look, she is making off with her mother's jewels."

Novella felt sick to her stomach – not just because she had her mother's jewels in the pillowcase, but because she could see that she would be spending the night locked up in her room.

'I wish the earth would swallow me up,' she moaned to herself, as they all stood there, enduring a tense silence.

Then at last the Officer spoke,

"I am sorry, sir, I cannot arrest this lady for taking her own mother's jewels. You told me that one of your horses had been stolen, which is why I came down to the Hall to investigate."

"But it was she who instigated the theft. She is in league with some local villain!"

Novella could only stand there with her mouth open.

"What nonsense is this?" she said wearily.

"Look, she has proven that she is a thief," continued Lord Buckton in high agitation as the poor Officer looked on in bewilderment.

"Sir, this is obviously a family matter and I cannot intervene on behalf of the law. Lady Novella is quite within her rights to take a horse if it is stabled on the premises and be in possession of her mother's jewels. Was not the Countess buried this very day?"

Lord Buckton looked at the man in horror. Novella could tell that he had not bargained for such a reaction.

"Yes, but I fail to see – " he stammered.

"I am sorry to have troubled you, my Lady, today of all days," said the Officer, humbly.

Then Lord Buckton spied the gun on the bed. Seizing it, a smile of triumph spread across his red face.

"What about her being in possession of a firearm? Is that not an offence?"

He caught up the gun in his hand and waved in the Officer's stunned face.

Novella did not know what possessed her at that moment, for she leapt at her stepfather and tried to take the gun off him.

"Give it to me! It is Mama's!" she screamed, as she lunged for the weapon.

But Lord Buckton was too strong and he caught Novella in a fierce grip. Holding her by the throat, he took the gun and aimed it squarely at her head.

"I will be rid of you once and for all, you darned nuisance!" he bawled.

"No! *No!*" cried Novella, as she saw his finger pull the trigger.

But Lord Buckton had not checked the safety catch – it was still quite firmly on and there was just a click from the pistol.

Novella swallowed hard, her legs shaking terribly. She had come within a hair's breadth of death and luck had been on her side.

Taking advantage of the fact that Lord Buckton's

attention was concentrated on the pistol and that he had slightly released his grip on her, Novella pulled away from him and dived behind the shocked Officer.

"Give that gun to me, sir," he demanded, but Lord Buckton paid no heed.

He was so far gone in his rage that he was beyond reason.

"Get out of my way, man! I'm going to shoot the little wretch and solve this problem once and for all!"

The Officer stepped forward with his hand out and as he did so, Lord Buckton took off the safety catch and shot him in the leg.

Falling to the ground with a yell, clutching his bleeding leg, the Officer could not have looked more astonished.

"Help! Help!" screeched Novella, feeling that she was surely next in line for a bullet.

But just as she began to shout even louder, the bedroom door flew open and in charged Sir Edward with a whole troop of Police Officers.

"Oh, my Heavens!" he cried, seeing the bleeding Officer on the floor. Within seconds, the Police had surrounded Lord Buckton and overpowered him.

The gun fell to the floor with a noisy clatter and Sir Edward ran to Novella who lay weeping on the bed.

"Darling, it is all over now," he said soothingly, as he cradled her in his arms. They embraced for a moment before turning towards the door just in time to see Lord Buckton being handcuffed and wrestled out of the room.

Two other Officers helped the wounded man to his feet. He was shaken but not badly injured.

"I will wait downstairs for you, Sir Edward," said the Officer in charge. "We will need to take statements from both of you shortly."

"Would you give us ten minutes, Officer? I want to make sure that Lady Novella is recovered enough to cope with your questions."

"Very good, sir" he replied, tactfully leaving the room.

As he left, Novella turned to Sir Edward, wonderment in her eyes.

"Edward, I do not understand how you knew I would be in danger?"

"After all you had told me, I guessed that your stepfather's absence meant only one thing – that he was up to no good at Crownley Hall. When you mentioned the people who had been looking around in droves, I believed that at worst, you might return home to find it overrun with more of them, so I decided to ask a friend of mine to arrange for some Police Officers to clear the scene. I had no idea how far in peril your life had become – it makes me terrified to think what might have happened had I not arrived when I did."

"But how did you get the Police to attend in such numbers?"

"By persuading my old friend, the Chief Constable – yes, the very same man who ensured that you reached Crownley Hall the day you returned from the school – that there would be an affray at the Hall. He was only too eager to help – it transpired that he was about to arrest Lord Buckton anyway for a number of frauds he had committed in London! He was in league with an actress – "

"Mrs. Byesouth!" gasped Novella,

"Most likely. The pair of them had defrauded several members of the aristocracy over some shady dealings with land and such. Now that he has added attempted murder to his list of felonies, I cannot see that he will be interfering with our lives for a long time to come."

"Look what I have found," said Novella, pulling open the pillowcase that lay beside her, "they are Mama's most precious jewels. I had thought they had all been sold."

"That is wonderful, Novella. We must put all of this behind us now and make plans for our future and Crownley Hall. That is all that matters."

"Do you mean you will help me restore it?" asked Novella, her eyes wide.

"As your father would have wished," he replied.

As he gently pulled her into his arms, Novella felt that she had never been so happy. Even though it was the day of her Mama's funeral, her future had gone from looking extremely bleak to being full of the most wonderful promise and love.

"Come, we should go downstairs," he urged. "I want to make sure that Lord Buckton does not escape justice this time."

Novella smiled, she could not believe how such a sad day had ended so well.

The pair of them walked hand in hand down the main staircase and watched as a howling Lord Buckton was bustled into the Police wagon that stood in the drive.

Mrs. Armitage was crying into her apron as the wagon drove off. She gave Novella a mournful stare – she knew that she would not be required for much longer at the Hall.

As the wagon pulled away into the distance, taking Lord Buckton out of their lives for ever, Sir Edward squeezed Novella's hand.

"Come, my darling. Let us walk around the garden – there is a beautiful sunset this evening."

And so it was. The sky was full of vivid pinks and blues – the clouds overhead high and soft. Novella watched the sun sink into the horizon with tears welling up in her eyes.

"Darling one?" asked Sir Edward, seeing her dab at her eyes.

"I am crying because I am so happy," she replied, "I feel as if Mama is at peace with Papa and that I now have only good times to look forward. Of course, I am sad that they will not be here to witness our wedding day, but I can only hope that, up in Heaven, they will know how lucky I am."

They watched in silence until the sky grew dark. Wrapping his arm around her shoulder, Sir Edward whispered,

"It will be another beautiful day tomorrow, my precious. Look at the sky. And it is the first day of the rest of our lives. We have only happiness to look forward to – and a life of love."

"Oh, Edward!" murmured Novella, as their lips met in a heavenly kiss.

Pulling back, her eyes were misty with passion and longing.

"My life for the past few years has been touched with tragedy and I felt as if I had nothing to live for when I returned to Crownley Hall.

"But now, through you, I have discovered that *love is the reason for living* – and we now have love in abundance. God has given us the great gift of loving and being loved and no gift could be more wonderful."

"The future is ours, my darling," replied Sir Edward, gently kissing her hair, "and with God's will and you by my side, love will see us through, whatever fate might bring."

Deep in her heart, Novella knew it was true. She had never before felt so completely loved.

"Together forever," she sighed, her smile full of love and adoration.

"Until the end of time!"